THE YOUNG COMMUNICATOR

By

S. D. L. WOOD

Copyright © S. D. L. Wood 2016
This book is sold subject to the condition that it shall not, by way of trade or otherwise, be lent, resold, hired out, or otherwise circulated without the publisher's prior consent in any form of binding or cover other than that in which it is published and without a similar condition including this condition being imposed on the subsequent publisher.
The moral right of S. D. L. Wood has been asserted.
ISBN-13: 978-1540585806
ISBN-10: 1540585808

For John and Doreen, with love.

CONTENTS

One	1
Two	7
Three	28
Four	62
Five	89
Six	101
Seven	110
Eight	130
Nine	143
Ten	175
Eleven	203
Twelve	218

ACKNOWLEDGMENTS

I am grateful to my family for their unwavering support and help. To Steve and Amelia for their belief in me and to George for his technical expertise and patience at my lack of it. Thanks also to Freddie and Louisa for their heart-warming responses to my original drafts, and to Buster for his positive feedback.

A special thank you to Julie James for her constant support and encouragement.

This is a work of fiction. Names, characters, businesses, organizations, places, events and incidents either are the product of the author's imagination or are used fictitiously. Any resemblance to actual persons, living or dead, events, or locales is entirely coincidental.

ONE

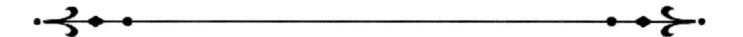

Cara didn't want to move. It didn't matter to her that it was, according to her mum, a good investment and had a bigger garden, she liked her house.

'What's wrong with our garden? What about my friends?' Cara had argued, when her mum Megan dropped the bombshell a few weeks previously.

'What about Dad? He's not even here. And what about Lily? Cats are very territorial and don't like moving, so she might even run away.'

Whilst she was saying all this, Cara could feel her emotions rising to the surface, like a dam about to burst its banks.

'Well, I won't go,' was Cara's parting shot as she flew out of the kitchen and up to her bedroom, slamming the door for added emphasis.

After a suitable cooling-off period, Megan gently knocked on Cara's bedroom door, then came in, and sat down on the edge of her bed, where she patiently tried to point out all of the advantages of moving house. Finally, she added that they had decided that their daughter could have the attic bedroom and promised that her father would decorate that room first on his return from the Middle East with the Army.

'Can I have some new bedroom furniture?' Cara asked, without relaxing her dour expression.

'I should think so,' her mother conceded.

Although Cara was still deeply unhappy about the situation, she felt she had won a slight victory.

'I'll think about it,' she replied.

*

Moving day came around all too quickly for Cara. Outside the weather was warm and sunny but inside, Cara felt cold and miserable, especially saying goodbye to her childhood home. At the new house, she wandered in and out of the different rooms with a heavy heart, trying to keep out of the way of the removal men with their heavy loads, thinking that her mum had greatly exaggerated its qualities; she thought the place just looked dirty and old fashioned. But worst of all, it didn't smell like home, just of someone else's.

She failed to see what her parents saw in the place.

Cara found the room which her mother agreed would be hers at the very top of the house; it had its own wooden staircase which opened into a large converted attic space which looked like it belonged to another time. The most noticeable feature being a dormer window, which looked out onto the untidy garden below. It also gave a good view of next door's; which by contrast, was immaculate. Opposite the stairs was a large cupboard built against one side of the sloping ceiling. But the most noticeable thing was the vivid olive-green carpet, complete with great big swirls in a slightly lighter shade.

Later, when the removal men had brought up the last of Cara's things and had assembled her bed, Megan appeared carrying the vacuum cleaner. Sensing her daughter's mood, she came over to give her a big hug.

'Isn't this exciting, darling?'

'I want to go home.'

'This is our home now, sweetie. I know it doesn't feel like it just yet, but you just have to try and imagine what it will look like when we have done it up. Just you wait – I know you will love it here.'

Cara wasn't convinced.

For the rest of the afternoon Cara busied herself making up her bed, unpacking and putting things where she wanted them. After the empty packing cases had been removed, she got to work with the vacuum cleaner. However, the ancient carpet didn't look any better from the experience.

One of the things Cara did like about the room, though, was the built-in cupboard; it was a good size, with lots of hanging space as well as some shelves, so it would make a great wardrobe. She attached the nozzle to the vacuum cleaner so she could get into the corners but, although there was enough room for her to stand up, Cara had to get onto her hands and knees to clean, as the floor of this cupboard was patched with an assortment of smaller bits of the same green carpet, like a bit of a jigsaw puzzle, and they didn't appear to be stuck down very well either, as pieces lifted with the suction. She was just about to replace a section, when she noticed a bit of paper sticking up between the wooden floor boards, and using the vacuum cleaner nozzle on it merely revealed that there was more of it.

She could simply have ignored it and replaced the bit of carpet and carried on cleaning, but curiosity stopped her. Instead, she switched off the vacuum and tried using her fingers to gently release it. It moved, but only slightly, though it was enough for her to see, even in the gloomy light, that there was something written on the paper. Worried that further pulling would tear it, she tried to lift the floor board next to it as it appeared to be broken and felt a bit loose. Cara then went in search of something she could use as a lever and found a ruler in her school pencil case which bent very quickly and soon broke under the strain. Using one of the broken parts, she dug under the board, and eventually succeeded in moving it sufficiently to reveal that the small piece of paper was in fact part of a sheet of paper and there looked to be quite a bit written on it.

Frustrated that she hadn't managed to lift the floor board completely, as it was held in place by a couple of nails along one side, Cara decided more drastic action was needed. Rushing downstairs, in the kitchen she found a sharp knife and managed to get it upstairs without her mother seeing. By levering this knife between the boards she eventually succeeded in lifting it, the wood giving a little sigh as it gave way, revealing a void underneath, containing what looked like a notebook. It was a loose page which had been sticking up, like some kind of flag, marking the spot.

Before she had a chance to examine her discovery, Cara heard her mother coming up the uncarpeted stairs, panting with the exertion of climbing two flights. She quickly re-covered the hole with a bit of carpet.

'Oh, it's quite a hike up here,' Megan said breathlessly. 'How are you getting on? I see you have made a very good start, well done,' she continued, casting an appreciative glance around Cara's bedroom. 'Auntie Jan and Uncle Ben have come over to help and they have brought some fish and chips, so come down now or they will be getting cold.'

Talk about bad timing, thought Cara. There was nothing for it but to go down with her mother. The treasure would have to wait.

TWO

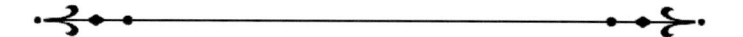

It was always good to see her aunt and uncle as they tended to make a fuss of her, especially Uncle Ben, who made an effort to spend time with Cara when her father was away on tour.

Whilst eating their fish and chips, they were asking her lots of questions about her plans for redecorating her bedroom, which normally she would have been happy to discuss in detail, but Cara just wanted to get back upstairs to examine her find. Not wishing to appear rude though, she answered their questions politely if almost monosyllabically.

Just before she left the table she asked to borrow a torch, explaining that there was no light in her wardrobe and she wanted to check that it was clean before she put her clothes in. Whilst her mum went to get the torch, Aunt Jan enquired how she was getting on up there and whether Cara would like any help sorting out her things, which was the last thing she wanted right now. So she replied that she could manage. Then taking the torch from her mother, she turned and trying not to look too eager, headed upstairs.

Back in her room, Cara was at last able to get a good look at the hidden gems under the floor board. The torch proved useful; as its light shone down into the void, she discovered that it was deeper than it first appeared, so was surprised to find not just one, but several old-fashioned note books. They reminded her of some of her dad's old school books he had shown her one day, which she had thought hilarious. These looked similar, perhaps a little smaller and with a hard front and back cover, which had been carefully covered in brown paper. Picking the topmost book, she blew the dust off, then could see a faint 'No. 1' drawn in black pen on the top. Fascinated, she turned the first few pages over and could tell from the way it was written, that this was someone's diary. Its author, she guessed was probably young, as the writing lacked the confident flourishes of an adult's. Flicking through, there were lots of entries, written in an assortment of different coloured pens.

Cara then picked up another note book, identical to the first, apart from 'No. 2' written on the front, again with black pen. Beneath that were more identical books, she counted four in total.

Sitting with her back resting against the open cupboard door, Cara felt a moment of unease, as she knew these diaries were somebody's private thoughts and wondered how she would feel if someone read her diary. These feelings, however, didn't last long, as curiosity overcame any pangs of guilt she might have felt as, after all, they were in her house, in her room, they had obviously been here a long time and had been forgotten about; so she was hardly going to get into any trouble, she thought.

Picking up the first diary and turning to the first entry dated July 20th, she expected it to be full of boring childish stuff about what they did on holiday. Little did she realise, that she would open up a world of strange phenomena she could never have imagined existed.

July 20th

A strange thing happened the other day. Mum had volunteered me to help clear out the old church hall, which was to be the temporary Scout hut until enough funds could be raised to build a new one. The original prefabricated structure caught fire during the annual Scout and Guides BBQ. The vicar then offered the use of an old building which had been the church hall many years ago; now it was used mainly as a store for church paraphernalia.

When Mum and I arrived, armed with our assortment of cleaning equipment, it looked like no one had crossed the threshold in years and my heart sank at the prospect of being stuck in there, especially as it was such a nice day. The place even seemed reluctant to let us enter. Mum had to put her shoulder to the door before it would open, releasing a strong odour of stale air, tinged with more than a hint of damp and decay. The windows were dressed with cobwebs and dust threads, hanging like funeral drapes for the host of dead flies lying on the windowsills and spilling onto the floor with their little legs in the air, as though they too found the musty smell too much to endure.

Mum, never fazed by such scenes, seemed to become somewhat energised and soon had the place sized up as she bustled about verbally organising her plan of campaign. A couple of ladies Mum knows had also been coerced into helping and they were quickly given their instructions, armed with cleaning equipment they were then dispatched to various corners before they had a chance to argue. I took this opportunity to sneak upstairs to have a bit of a snoop around, but Mum caught me.

'Where do you think you are going?'

'I thought I might start upstairs.'

'Ok, but make sure you do a proper job!'

Upstairs was one big room which thankfully wasn't as cluttered as downstairs. There were a few large tea chests, full of what looked like mostly papers and an old desk stuffed with even more bits of paper, a lot of which had tumbled onto the floor. To one side of the desk were a few neatly stacked piles of old hymn sheets; otherwise it was just very dusty.

It didn't take me too long to clear the floor of rubbish. I arranged the papers in the desk tidily and swept the floor. I was just picking up a stray matchbox when Mum called up the stairs to say that they were having a tea break. I turned around and threw the matchbox into the bulging black bag of rubbish which was propped up in the opposite corner, congratulating myself that I had aimed well, and then turned for the stairs. I hadn't got very far, when I heard a 'plop' noise behind me. Turning around, I saw what looked like the same matchbox, so I picked it up and had a look at it this time before throwing it in the bin bag. I waited a moment or two before turning to walk to the stairs once again and almost at once I heard the 'plop' noise again to my left and there was the matchbox. When I picked it up and could see it was the same one, so I turned back to look around the room – I don't know why because I was the only person there, then I put the matchbox in my pocket and went downstairs for a drink.

'How much more do you have to do up there?' Mum asked.

'Not much, just dust the surfaces,' I informed her.

'Good. We are just about finished down here so I will give you a hand.'

After we had finished our tea, I made my way up the creaky wooden stairs but, as I neared the top, I stopped dead in my racks, hardly believing the scene in front of me. The floor, which minutes earlier I had swept clear, was now littered with bits of paper. Some were torn into tiny pieces, others left as whole pages of old hymn sheets. There looked to be hundreds of them scattered all over the floor. Eerily, the black bag which I had left packed with rubbish, was now hanging empty, suspended from the ceiling, its edges tied to the central ceiling light. It resembled a huge black lampshade, the light bulb inside was on and cast a dull diffused glow over the carnage below it, the whole thing swayed gently as though caught in a draught, despite the fact that there were no windows open.

As I stood surveying the chaos, I could hear Mum's footsteps coming up the stairs. My heart beat faster at the thought of what to say. I knew she would go bananas. I was frozen to the spot as she drew level with me. I heard her sharp intake of breath as she stood motionless beside me. I could almost sense her anger as she exhaled wearily, then walked into the room and reached up to grab the black bag from the light fitting with such force I thought the whole thing would come away from the ceiling, leaving two ends behind, attached just above the bulb so that it resembled a white rabbit with two black ears.

'Do you need any help up there?' one of the ladies shouted up from below.

'No, we're fine, thanks,' Mum politely replied, then, noticeably less so to me, she said: 'Switch that light off, Suzann, and go and get another black bag and brush, will you?'

It took both of us about ten minutes to clear up the mess. During that time Mum didn't say a word but, then again neither did I. What could I say? She would not believe me. As we were leaving, carrying equipment and the bag of rubbish downstairs, I turned around to make sure we hadn't left anything. When, out of the corner of my eye, I saw him – a young boy dressed in old fashioned shorts and sleeveless jumper, sitting on top of the desk – he was smiling cheekily at me.

When we got home, I shut myself in my room, hoping Mum would soon forget about it. I don't suppose she will pay me anything for helping, as she said she would, and I don't really feel like reminding her either. Why do these things always happen to me?

*

Cara put the book down after reading that entry, feeling puzzled. What was this all about? She wondered. Was it a school assignment? An exercise in imaginary creative writing perhaps? Whatever it was, the writer had taken the trouble to incorporate careful descriptions that made it seem very visual and almost real, Cara thought. But what did it mean? She felt compelled to read on.

21 July

I could feel the sunshine gently warming my face long before I opened my eyes. Then the fleeting confusion, as I tried to work out what day it was, and slowly, the realisation dawned that this wasn't a school day, in fact it was the first day of the school holidays and six long weeks lay ahead of me! Breathing a contented sigh and snuggling deeper under the covers, I opened one eye and then the other to see the sun streaming through the small gap in my curtains. I glanced at the alarm clock on my bedside table, which Phil – our lodger – had hurriedly put together one afternoon and not yet finished. The door and drawer handles were missing and half of it was without a coat of paint, but then it fitted in with the rest of my room quite well in that respect. Half my room retained its pink theme. Tiny rose bud wallpaper covered half the walls and a pale primrose colour on the remaining walls, another of Phil's 'projects'. The pattern on my curtains was of little pink fairies and toadstools, remnants of my younger days. The furniture too was a bit of a mismatch, some pieces bare pine, others painted cream. My room, like me, was in transition, no longer a child but not yet an adult.

My alarm clock read 8.05am, so I turned over, happy in the knowledge that there was nothing I needed to get up for. Below my window I could hear Phil's habitual whistling in the garden as he tended his produce, all perfectly formed specimens growing in neat regimented rows.

Phil came to live with us, by accident really, about six years ago. Mum had advertised for a lodger, as she was finding money a bit tight after the divorce.

She then placed an advert in the local paper but after a few initial enquiries she didn't find anyone 'suitable'. Just as she had given up all hope of finding someone, the phone rang and, by the end of the call Phil had managed to persuade Mum to let him come for an interview.

During the past few years Mum has told me in no uncertain terms, about the impression he made on her at the time, which I gather wasn't very favourable. I know she finds him exasperating at times, I usually find it amusing as they really are total opposites in every respect, but surprisingly, their relationship works quite well.

I believe the reason that Phil won Mum over was by complimenting her on the house – her pride and joy. But I think the thing that must have clinched it for Phil was that he had said how 'handy' he was and that he was a gardener by trade. Knowing how much Mum dislikes gardening and dealing with maintenance problems, I can imagine her calculating the advantages of having Phil as our lodger. Mum looks after things inside the house and Phil looks after all things outside. The garden has been transformed from a barren featureless patch to one which many would envy. His vegetables are a sight to behold, row upon neat regimented row, all perfectly formed, which have won him many a prize in local shows. He certainly has 'green fingers' but their powers do not extend to DIY; I have lost count of the number of jobs he's started and not got around to finishing. Phil is definitely an outdoors sort of person. He does gardening jobs for people in our village, works part time at the garden centre, as well as helping out at Durley Manor, which is just on the outskirts of the village, as well as doing our own garden.

Moments later, I was jolted from my daydreams, by Mum shouting up the stairs. The sense of urgency in her voice made me sit up immediately.

'Suzann! Suzann, have you forgotten you are going with Phil this morning? Come on or you will be late,'

Mum said breathlessly as she burst into my room.

'He's going in a few minutes,' she continued, going over to draw back my curtains.

'I'm off now, so I'll see you later. There's some ham in the fridge, but I'll be back before you, no doubt.' And with that she turned and disappeared the way she had come. She was right. I had forgotten.

Fifteen minutes later we were on our way to Durley Manor, rolling along in Phil's ancient Citroen, or 'mobile shed', as Mum calls it. Looking at it, I could understand why. Tools of all shapes and sizes littered the back seat and every other surface was covered with a thin layer of compost. Mum refuses to travel in it anymore after she found that she had been sitting on a worm for an entire journey!

The Manor is just about a twenty-minute drive from our house, just outside of the village, where it nestles amid lush rolling hills interspersed with ancient woodland – so typical of our county. The start of the estate is marked by a dilapidated wrought iron gate, which looks as if it hasn't moved for decades. It had obviously been one of a pair, but its partner was missing. Just inside the gateway on the right stood what must have been, at one time, a rather nice gatehouse, with exposed timbers and stone mullioned windows, but the glass was missing; the windows and door were now boarded up, and ivy curled around the stone into cracks and crevices.

The long private drive to the Manor reminded me of a fairground ride, although a bit bumpier. The drive was full of potholes the size of small ponds. Although Phil was practiced at avoiding the worst of them, he seemed oblivious to the rest, as we swayed and lurched our way past vast banks of rhododendrons, which stood either side of the drive and were so tall that they almost seemed to meet at the top.

From a distance, the sight of Durley Manor could almost take your breath away, especially having survived the claustrophobic drive. The house sat regally in an immense stretch of lawn and was a mixture of different styles, some of which I recognised, others not. It had exposed timbers on the upper parts, stone on lower parts and what looked like later brick additions. As we got closer, you could see that it looked a bit neglected. Ivy covered large sections and was creeping upwards towards the huge Jacobean chimneys, which the sagging roof looked ill-equipped to support.

Phil drove around the side of the house to the old

brick built stable block, and into the central cobbled courtyard. He had brought me along today on the pretext of letting me see some kittens, but I suspect that Mum wasn't happy about me being left on my own all day, which is fine because I am potty about animals, and I couldn't resist an opportunity to see the Manor.

*

We found the kittens quite easily; they were in a large cardboard box, snuggled up to their mum on an old towel. There were three of them, one white and ginger, one all ginger and one tortoise shell. Phil told me they were four weeks old and I thought they were absolutely adorable. I bent to stroke the mother and then the kittens. So absorbed was I that I didn't notice that someone had joined us until I heard a posh voice say, 'You can have one when they are old enough to leave their mother, if you would like?'

Turning around I saw a boy who must have been about my age standing next to Phil.

'Hello Hugo,' Phil said. 'This is Suzann; I've brought her along to see the kittens as she's nuts about animals. Anyway, I'd best be off. Is your dad about?'

'Yes, he's in the house – he's expecting you.'

'Right. I'll see you later, Suz.'

And with that he turned and left me with Hugo.

Hugo came a bit nearer and then bent down to stroke the kittens, which enabled me to sneak a glance in his direction. He had thick dark hair, which, in the shade of the stables, looked nearly black. It was cut in what my mum would call a conventional style, unlike the boys I knew, who sported the latest craze. It was obvious that Hugo didn't attend my school, not simply due to the fact that I had not seen him there, but because none of the boys I knew spoke as nicely as he did.

'Which one do you like the best?' Hugo asked.

'I'm not sure, they're all gorgeous... but I suppose this one is quite cute,' I replied, gently picking up the ginger kitten and holding it in the palm of my hand.

'Then that is the one you must have.'

'Thank you, but I will have to check with my mum first,' I said, as I reluctantly returned it to its mother.

We both watched the kittens sprawling over their mother for a few moments and then he suddenly got to his feet.

'So, you like animals, do you?'

'Yes, I do,' I replied, also rising to my feet.

'Would you like to see some horses?'

'OK,' I said, taking one more look at the kittens.

We walked out of the stable block and out across the large expanse of lawn at the back of the house, in the centre of which stood what must have been quite an elaborate fountain, only there was no water in it. It too was showing distinct signs of neglect with a number of large cracks visible and sections of stone broken off or damaged. I stopped to lean against the base of the fountain because I had a stone in my shoe, and I felt the need to break the silence, so I asked a few polite questions about the house. As I admired the rear of the house, he told me that he lived there alone with his father. I was surprised to discover that they only lived in a relatively small portion of the house, but Hugo told me that it was too expensive to heat, clean and maintain the whole building. I thought to myself that if I had a house this big, I'd make sure that I lived in the whole of it, sleep in a different room every night. Apparently it had twenty-two bedrooms – TWENTY-TWO! Obviously, I tried to look cool about this when he told me, like it was normal to have that many rooms.

The back of the house looked a bit more impressive than the front. All the windows were roughly similar and there wasn't too much ivy growing everywhere. There was a row of French windows which led out onto a kind of long terrace with steps leading down to the lawn. Above the French doors was a large window where I distinctly saw the figure of a young woman stood looking down at us.

'Did you say your housekeeper lives with you?'

'No, she lives in the village with her husband Tom Burgess, who sometimes helps out.'

Wondering who it was that I had seen at the window, I asked Hugo how long Mrs Burgess had worked for his father and he told me that she had been with the family for about fourteen years. The young woman I had seen looked not that many years older than me, so it obviously wasn't the housekeeper.

As we continued our walk, Hugo told me a little about his school, a private school about thirty miles from here, so he only comes home during the holidays. I asked him whether he missed his home much.

'Sometimes, but I've been at the school since I was eight, so it becomes your home. The only problem is that my friends all live a long way from here and I don't get to meet people my own age, from the village.'

We arrived at the paddock where three chestnut

horses were grazing. Hugo made a kind of clucking noise and immediately they looked in our direction and started to saunter over towards us. Hugo rummaged in one of his pockets and produced a few pieces of carrot which he offered to them on an outstretched, flattened palm. At the sight of this treat the horses quickened their pace and jostled for position, one getting slightly impatient and giving one of the horses who was nearer to Hugo a bit of a nip on the neck.

'That's my horse, Lancelot; he likes to be the boss, even though he's the baby of them. This is Genevieve and the other one is Flame.'

They looked very well cared for, their coats looked immaculately groomed and they exuded health and vitality.

'Do you ride?' Hugo asked.

I hesitated, as I wasn't sure what to say. It was true that I had ridden but then it was over five years ago. Mum had a friend in the village that had a few horses and she gave me lessons, but I had no natural talent for horse riding. In fact, Mary, Mum's friend, often remarked that I looked like 'a sack of potatoes' on a horse. To be honest, although I did quite enjoy it, sometimes, I have to admit I was scared witless.

'Not very well,' I answered truthfully.

'I could give you a few lessons if you would like? You could come over when Phil's working here, I'm sure we can find a riding hat to fit you.'

'That would be great, but I will have to check with my mum first.' It did sound a good opportunity and Mum could hardly object as it wasn't going to cost anything.

We then walked back to the main house and met up with Phil outside the stable block. He was talking to a rather portly man dressed in tweeds with leather patches at the elbows. He reminded me of an expensive but old fashioned, upholstered chair; although not yet an antique, it was difficult to guess his age. The most striking thing about him was his great handlebar moustache which practically joined his sideburns. To complete this 'Country Life' scene, two dogs lay at his feet, Labradors, I think, one golden, the other black.

Phil introduced me to him, I mumbled a shy, 'Hello,' and that was that. Phil and I got into his old Citroen and we rumbled off down the drive. As we did so, something made me turn and look back at the house.

Was it a trick of the light, or was the girl I had seen earlier watching me from one of the upstairs windows?

I didn't bother to ask Phil if he could see anyone because I knew the answer to that already.

*

'Cara…' Cara heard her mother step on the creaky bottom step, thankful that it provided an early warning when someone was on their way up; it gave her sufficient time to put the diaries back where they had come from, before Meg got to the top of the stairs.

'I think I need to get back to the gym!' she said, slightly out of breath. 'I just wanted to remind you about your Skype call with your dad.'

Cara had been so engrossed in Suzann's world; she had forgotten all about the call.

'Come on, get your skates on.'

They soon got her computer set up and ready to make the connection, Cara feeling a bit guilty, as normally she couldn't wait to speak to her dad, especially as it didn't happen as often as she would like.

It felt good to speak to him; reassuringly, he looked and sounded the same as ever. Naturally, a lot of the talk was about the new house and Cara did her best to sound happy about things because she didn't want him to worry about her, as there was nothing he could do about it, being so many thousands of miles away. He too sounded as pleased as Meg was about the move and his plans for renovating it when he returned but, that was three months away.

As usual, after she had said, 'Goodbye,' she felt an overwhelming sadness envelop her, so that first night, the diaries were temporarily forgotten. She missed her dad and her old home and sensed that her life was changing but felt somehow powerless to do anything to steer its course. Like a leaf caught on the wind, she just had to trust it was going in the right direction for her.

THREE

After a poor night's sleep, filled with dreams that made no sense, involving strange people she did not recognise, Cara woke feeling tired.

Getting up, she drew back the makeshift curtains, which barely reached the windowsill and clashed hideously with the green carpet and peach wallpaper. She looked out at a clear blue sky, it looked like it was going to be a nice day, then she remembered that her friend Alicia was coming over. It seemed to Cara that she had not seen her for weeks, when it was actually only five days ago, on the last day of the school year. She felt she had so much to tell her friend but, was still undecided whether to share her discovery with her just yet.

*

Shortly after breakfast Alicia arrived, accompanied

by her warm, effervescent energy, which she seemed to have difficulty containing; it fairly fizzed out of her, like a shaken lemonade bottle upon opening.

No sooner had Alicia given her best friend a hug, she insisted on being given a tour of the house. Cara, although unenthusiastic, obliged but was a little disappointed in Alicia's enthusiastic response; she was especially keen on Cara's room, saying how envious she was of Cara having a whole floor to herself. But that was Alicia; she had the knack of saying all the right things, at the right time to the right people, especially when they needed cheering up.

The two girls made themselves comfy on the bed, with Lily curled up between them, enjoying her morning nap. They caught up on end-of-term gossip, the latest apps, and discussed plans for the rest of summer holidays. Alicia had just moved on to talk about who was going to be in her history group in the autumn term, when Cara, on the spur of the moment, decided to confide in her.

'Ali, what would you do if you found someone's diary? Would you read it?'

'I'm not sure, it would depend on whose it was. If it was someone I knew, then definitely not, as I wouldn't want anybody reading mine.'

'What if you just found it and had no idea whose it was?'

'Well, I suppose the only way to find out who it belongs to would be to read it, as presumably, they would be pleased to get it back. Why do you ask? Have you found one?' Alicia asked whilst absentmindedly tickling one of Lily's paws as she slept.

'Yes.'

'Oh, where did you find it?'

'Here,' Cara replied. 'In this house.'

'Really?' Alicia sat up, giving Cara her full attention. 'Where?'

'In my wardrobe, under the floor boards.'

'No! Show me.'

Cara led her towards the built-in wardrobe when she suddenly stopped on hearing the now familiar creak of the bottom step, then moments later, Megan appeared.

'Hi girls. What you up to?'

'Cara was just showing me—'

'My lovely wardrobe,' Cara quickly cut in whilst giving Alicia a bit of a nudge.

'Yes, she's a lucky girl, isn't she?' Megan replied,

smiling at her daughter's first positive comment about the house. 'It's bigger than mine. Now, I've made some sandwiches for lunch, so if you would like to come down now, as I thought we could go out this afternoon. I am fed up with unpacking and it is such a nice day. I thought we could go shopping for some bits and pieces for your bedroom, Cara. With Alicia's help we might get some nice things.'

'Great. We will be down in a minute, Mum.'

After they were sure Megan was out of earshot, Cara apologised to Alicia for nudging her.

'I haven't told anyone but you about what I have found,' Cara explained.

'Why not?'

'Oh, you know what parents are like. Mum will probably take it away before I have had a chance to read it. She will probably say it's not suitable reading material. I don't know, perhaps I will tell her but not before I have read them and, I have only just found them.'

Cara quickly showed her friend where she had made her discovery before they heard Meg's voice calling for them to come down.

'Come on, I'll show you them later.'

'Them. You mean there's more than one?' Alicia

replied, eyes wide with excitement.

'Four altogether, but remember, this is our little secret.'

After lunch, the girls accompanied by Meg went to the out-of-town shopping centre, where they spent a happy afternoon looking at all things bedroom related. Alicia was a great help to her friend in this matter, as she had a good eye for colour, and enjoyed anything to do with interior design, and loved pretty things.

They didn't get an opportunity to talk about the diaries until they had stopped for a coffee. Whilst Meg was at the counter placing their orders, Alicia made the most of her absence to ask Cara whether she could read a bit before her dad came to pick her up. Cara replied that there might be enough time if they didn't spend much more time shopping. As a result of this conversation, Alicia's enthusiasm for the shopping excursion cooled considerably, which Meg picked up on, so she suggested they call it a day and return home.

Back in Cara's attic bedroom, her friend could hardly wait to look at the diaries. When they were brought out of their secret hiding place, Alicia handled them as carefully as if they had been precious works of art. Glancing at each one, turning them over slowly, she even smelt them.

'You can just smell the age, can't you?' she said, reminding Cara of her dad mimicking wine connoisseurs, when offered a glass of something.

'Which one have you started reading?'

Cara explained, that she thought it best to read them in chronological order, otherwise things wouldn't make sense.

Alicia then took up her position on the bed, propped up with cushions and started to read until she got to the point where Cara had reached.

'Well, what do you think?' Cara was anxious to know, after Alicia had put the diary down.

'I don't know. It's a bit odd, isn't it? How old do you think they are?'

'You can tell they are pretty old by the way they look but it's difficult to say.'

'Who do you think this Suzann is? I mean do you think she is a real person?' Alicia asked, feeling genuinely intrigued by what her friend had discovered.

'I don't think so. It looks more like a school assignment in creative writing to me.'

'Some assignment,' Alicia said, looking at the other diaries spread out on the bed. 'There's a lot of it and it is written as a diary.'

'Well I suppose the more we read the more we will find out,' Cara suggested.

'Absolutely,' Alicia replied. 'This is quite exciting, shall we read the next chapter together? We might find out a bit more.'

The two made themselves comfortable and turned to the next entry dated 24th July.

'Look at that!' Alicia said, pointing to the date. 'That's today's date.'

24th July

The smell of warm toast wafting upstairs was enough to prise me out of bed – I was hungry. In the kitchen, Mum was making toast and Phil had just popped in from the garden with a couple of bundles of carrots, which he had clearly just dug from the garden. He was sheepishly trying to discard his earthy boots without scattering too much dirt all over the kitchen floor. No doubt he was hoping Mum hadn't noticed as some of the mud splattered up the sides of the wall. She hadn't missed it and cast him a look, which we both knew meant, 'You had better get that cleaned up.' Phil produced a handkerchief, which must once have been white, and used this to wipe up the offending mess. No doubt in an attempt at distraction, he asked if we had heard the latest gossip.

'There's been another burglary in the village.'

'Oh!' said Mum. 'Not another. Who this time?'

'Up at the Major's place. Took some silver, from what I heard. A fair amount was taken, although they didn't take everything – looks like they are a bit choosey.'

'Oh dear, poor Major Thomas. I hope they didn't make a mess,' Mum said.

I could sense her concern as she was probably thinking of the part she would have to play in helping to clear it all up, as she cleaned for the Major and Mrs Thomas.

'Yeah, a right mess apparently.'

Was he winding Mum up?

'Why do they have to make such a mess? If they want the silver, take it but leave everything else alone.' Phil had clearly succeeded, as she was whipping herself into a right mood. She snatched my mug from me even though I hadn't quite finished, and took away

Phil's plate, leaving him to finish eating his toast at the risk of dropping his crumbs on the bare table.

Mum clattered about in the kitchen whilst Phil and I silently finished our breakfast. Phil's attempts to defuse the situation caused by his mess on the kitchen floor had backfired, and I could sense that he wanted to get back to his garden. This was probably the best place for him right now. As Mum opened one of the kitchen cupboards, which Phil was supposed to have repaired, it swung out awkwardly, as the top hinge was missing.

'And just when do you think we could get this sorted, Mr DIY? It's driving me mad.'

'I'm working on it,' Phil said, with a mouth full of toast, whilst backing out of the door and putting his muddy boots back on at the same time.

Mum knew it was futile to say any more and simply sighed as he slammed the kitchen door behind him.

Just then the phone rang and Mum disappeared into the hall. Phil then reappeared, poking his head around the kitchen door without setting foot inside.

'Forgot to mention, Hugo asked if you would like to go riding tomorrow. I will be going about ten if you want to come.'

'Yes, OK,' I said, before I had time to think about it.

There wasn't much going on today. Mum said she had to pop out for a bit this morning, as it was her day to clean up at the doctor's house. She would be at least a couple of hours. Phil disappeared about ten o'clock to do one of his jobs, so I had the house to myself for a while. I quite like having the house to myself, it feels like it's all mine, although the house kind of takes on a different atmosphere and it is quiet and peaceful. I went upstairs to get my book, which I had nearly finished reading and whilst up there I decided to tidy my bedroom, when pulling back the curtains, I saw Maud, our elderly next door neighbour, out in her garden. Something made me stop and watch her for a few minutes, as she seemed to be wandering aimlessly, as though slightly confused or disorientated. I watched her, dressed in a familiar tweed skirt she seemed so fond of, as she slowly meandered down her garden path which dissects the long stretch of lawn. The small flower borders on each side are kept neat and tidy by Archie, her husband. He too is a keen gardener, but no competition for Phil. Maud stopped to look at a few of the flowers, bending as though to smell their scent but then, seemingly deciding against it, she made her way down towards the end of the path. At this point my interest was drawn back to my book. I took it downstairs and got myself comfy in my favourite part of the sofa, to lose myself in the story.

After a while I went to get myself a drink from the kitchen. When I went in, there was Maud standing by the door.

'Hello,' I said. 'If you are looking for Mum she's gone around to the doctor's house, she shouldn't be too long.'

Maud often popped in. Both she and Archie have been good neighbours and a help to Mum as well, especially when I was younger and Mum needed someone to babysit. Now they are getting on a bit, Mum looks out for them.

'Would you like a cup of tea while you wait? I'm just making one.'

I turned and busied myself getting mugs out of the cupboard, although she still hadn't told me whether she wanted one or not. Turning back to her, I could see that something wasn't quite right. I was just about to ask her if anything was the matter, when she looked straight at me and said something rather odd.

'Tell Archie, he will find the papers he needs in the green suitcase in the loft. I put them there for safe keeping.'

Not knowing quite how to reply to that, I turned back to making the tea. I started to ask her if she would like a biscuit, and when she didn't answer, I swung round to find that there was no one there and I hadn't heard the door open or shut.

Mum got back about an hour later. The front door slammed and I heard the familiar tread of her sensible work shoes on the tiled hall floor as she made her way to the kitchen, then the click of the kettle switch and clatter of mug and spoon as she made herself a cup of tea. *Does she know?* I wondered. *And if so, shall I go in now, or do I wait for her to come to me?* I decided to wait. After about five minutes Mum came into the sitting room. One look at her face revealed what I needed to know and now I would know what to do and say.

'Is something the matter, Mum?'

'It's a sad day, I'm afraid, Suzann. A sad day... Maud died this morning, about an hour or so ago. The doctor rushed down here and broke the news to me when he got back. I was too upset to do any more work, so he drove me home. I must pop round and see Archie, see if there is anything I can do, poor man.'

*

'The mystery deepens,' Alicia said, after they had finished reading. 'It's a bit weird, don't you think?'

Cara couldn't help but agree with her.

'Do you know what I think?' Alicia announced, sitting up straight. 'I think she might be one of those people who can see ghosts or spirits. Do you remember that programme on TV, I think it was an American thing, where this guy told people all sorts of things nobody could possibly know, because he was able to talk to their dead relatives? I can't remember what it was called.'

'No, I don't think I watched that. And they are called psychics or mediums.'

'Yeah, that's right. My mum is quite interested in that sort of thing but, my dad thinks it's all a load of rubbish.'

Just then, Alicia's phone buzzed, which told her that her dad had arrived to pick her up.

'I had better go. Copy me the next chapter, will

you?'

As they were saying their goodbyes, Meg asked if Alicia would like to come over again tomorrow.

'I thought Cara and I could do with a fun day away from unpacking and go and see the local stately home as it's just up the road. It has recently reopened after having some renovations, so it should be quite interesting to see. There is a café there too, so I will treat you to lunch?'

'That sounds good,' Alicia's dad replied. 'Can I come? I don't think we have anything planned for tomorrow.'

'Is it Durley Manor?' Cara asked.

'Yes, that's right,' Meg replied, pleasantly surprised at her daughter's local knowledge. 'What do you think, girls?'

The two friends exchanged surprised glances.

'I think it's a wonderful idea,' Alicia replied, her eyes twinkling with excitement.

*

Later, before going to sleep, Cara copied and sent the next instalment in Suzann's diary to Alicia, then settled down to read it herself.

25th July

Phil and I left at around 10am and soon we were trundling down the narrow lane to Durley Manor. *It's a good job,* I thought to myself as we swayed and bumped along, *that I don't suffer from travel sickness!* The constant, although mild, smell of compost didn't help either, so I was quite glad when we arrived at the main entrance to the Manor.

Hugo's father looked to be saying goodbye to a man dressed in a smart suit. He was followed by the two dogs.

'Ah, Philip my boy.' He greeted us as we got out of the car, and the dogs came over to us. 'Lots to do today, lots to do. I see you have brought along your little helper again, eh?'

'No, Squire. Suzann has come at Hugo's invitation,' Phil replied, patting both dogs in turn.

'Has she by Jove, well well. Hugo's in the house. Pop along and see Mrs Burgess. She's in the kitchen; she'll give you some of her nice biscuits, if you're lucky.'

I made my way through the huge stone arched

porch, which wouldn't have looked out of place in a cathedral, and into the spectacular hall, the sight of which nearly took my breath away. The walls were lined with wooden panelling to roughly the height of a tall man; above, the walls were painted in a light colour but covered with numerous swords, spears and shields, all of which were arranged in decorative patterns. Above this was the ceiling which was vaulted, revealing exposed wooden beams which were the same colour as the wooden panelling below and from which cartwheel-sized lights were hung. At one end of the hall was a large stone fireplace, which looked as if it had been used recently, as there was ash and half burnt wood in the grate. Either side of the fireplace stood a full suit of armour, complete with helmet and spear. In the centre of the wall, above the fireplace, a stag's head with enormous antlers was mounted. Even from a distance, it looked like it had seen better days – it was a bit torn and battered and caked in dust from the fire below. Towards the other end of the room an elaborately carved wooden staircase rose from the black and white chequered marble floor, which was dotted with a couple of colourful but well-worn rugs. The wide staircase led to a long galleried landing, along which hung numerous portraits, in heavy gilt frames, of what I presumed to be the family's ancestors.

'Oh, there you are, my dear.' A lady, wearing a brightly coloured plastic apron approached from the door at the far end of the hall. 'It's Suzann, isn't it? Hugo has been expecting you. Come this way, he's in the kitchen.'

I followed this small but sprightly lady who looked a bit older than my mum, out of the hall and into a small stone-floored passage, which led to the kitchen. And what a kitchen! You could have put the whole of our downstairs into this room. The fireplace was nearly as big as a small bedroom. Cupboards ran all the way along the wall opposite the door and a big dresser took up much of the adjacent wall, which had brightly coloured plates and dishes displayed along its shelves, together with an array of letters, cards, books and the odd photograph. In the centre of the kitchen was a rather ancient-looking long wooden table where Hugo was sitting, tucking into a rather delicious-looking piece of chocolate cake.

Hugo looked up and motioned for me to sit down opposite him. He was unable to speak because he had his mouth full of cake.

'Would you like a piece of cake, my dear?' Mrs Burgess asked, setting a generous portion in front of me before I had time to reply.

'Thank you.'

'Glad you could make it,' Hugo said.

'Thank you for inviting me,' I replied between mouthfuls.

After we had satisfied ourselves with Mrs Burgess's yummy cake, Hugo asked if I would like a 'free' tour of the house. I replied 'yes', as casually as I could, trying to hide my excitement and curiosity.

Hugo's tour started in the Hall, which, he explained was the original banqueting hall, built around the end of the seventeenth century. Looking around, it wasn't hard to imagine it. I asked if the suits of armour either side of the fireplace were original too and was disappointed to learn that they were bought in France in the 1930s. Hugo seemed very knowledgeable about the house and spoke enthusiastically as he pointed out various past members of his family whose portraits lined the walls of the stairs and gallery beyond.

He led me from one room to another. The morning room, the snug and the study, which he told me, was a later addition to the house. This room appealed to me the most. It wasn't very big compared with the other rooms we had seen, but it looked more cosy, with two comfy-looking sofas and French windows which led out on to the garden at the back. The room was lined with bookshelves from floor to ceiling along three walls, the shorter one had a smallish fire place set into the middle with shelves either side of it.

'There's a secret in this room,' Hugo said almost smugly. 'I bet you can't spot it.'

'Is it a secret passage?' I asked.

'I'm not saying anything – you tell me.'

I looked around the room and my eyes felt drawn to the smaller bookcase to the right of the fireplace. I went over and ran my fingers along the spines of the many books, which were real enough – not false ones set in to look like books. Turning to look at Hugo, I could see that he was smiling a little.

'You're very warm, do you give in?'

'OK.'

He came over to where I was standing, and half pulled out a book with a blue sleeve entitled, 'The Unwelcome Guest'. Suddenly there was the noise of wood scraping upon wood, and then the bookcase opened inward from the right, to reveal a dark unlit passage.

'Wow... that's amazing!' I said, breathing in a strong, musty, damp smell as I peered into the gloom. 'Where does that go?'

'It leads to the scullery, next to the kitchen. Many people believe that the passage led into the village, but we can't prove it as the roof must have caved in at some time, so it's blocked just after the scullery door. Father says that I haven't to use it, as he thinks it's unsafe... but I do. I hide from Mrs B sometimes, it's fun. Do you want to try it out?'

I didn't fancy it much, I must say, especially as there was a chance that it was dangerous. The passage didn't look that appealing – cold and damp.

'How can we? It's so dark in there. Are there any lights?'

'Don't be silly, electricity hadn't been invented when this was built. I use a torch. I've got one which I keep in here especially.' He reached into the cupboard beneath one of the bookcases and brought out a large torch, which he tested by shining it in my face.

'Thanks!' I said, turning my face away from him.

'Just testing. Are you game then?' Without waiting for a reply, Hugo stepped into the passage ahead of me.

'Hey! Just a minute. How do we get out at the other end?' I asked, trying not to seem overly anxious.

'That's easy, there's a handle we pull. Come on, I've done it hundreds of times... you're not scared, are you?' Hugo turned to check for any signs of fear.

'Of course not,' I lied and, against my better judgement, stepped into the darkness.

'Close the door after you.'

The bookcase door was surprisingly heavy. It made a slight 'click' as it shut tightly, leaving us both in total darkness, except for the single beam of the torch. Hugo was already walking ahead of me. It was impossible for me to see what was beneath my feet, so I had to stretch my arms out to touch the cold, clammy and uneven surface of the passage walls.

'Wait up... you're going too fast, I can't see where I am going.'

'Sorry,' Hugo said, turning back and shining the torch down at the ground so I could see what lay immediately in front of me.

'The ground is perfectly level, so you needn't worry.'

We walked for a few minutes, Hugo just slightly in front of me, as the tunnel wasn't wide enough to allow us to walk side by side. Our path wasn't as straight as I had imagined it would be. I was gradually beginning to feel less uneasy in these strange surroundings, as my eyes became adjusted to the gloom. Hugo, I sensed, appeared confident and perfectly relaxed. Then all of a sudden we were plunged into complete darkness.

I let out an involuntary gasp and instinctively reached out for Hugo, grabbing his arm and holding on tightly.

'Oh blast... the stupid battery's gone,' Hugo said, surprisingly calmly.

'What do you mean it's gone?' I replied, in a voice that sounded alarmingly high-pitched.

'Sorry, the battery is flat, can't do anything about it right now, but we haven't far to go. Here, hold my hand, and I will lead the way. Remember, I've done this loads of times. There's nothing to worry about.'

All I kept thinking about was that I bet Hugo had done this on purpose, that it was some sort of test that he was no doubt finding really amusing. Well I wasn't going to give him the satisfaction of thinking I was scared. So I released my grip on Hugo's hand as he led me deeper into the dark tunnel to goodness knows where, my heart beating so wildly I didn't know how Hugo could fail to hear it. We continued our progress, although at a much slower pace. I held out my right arm to touch the wall for support, which felt rough and dirty. I also felt cobwebs against my skin and just hoped there were no spiders in them.

After what seemed like a very long time, but was probably only a few minutes, Hugo stopped. I heard him moving his hands over a surface and fumbling with something.

'Here we are...'

I heard a 'click' and then saw, with a certain amount of relief, a dazzling crack of light which got bigger and bigger as a door opened. Moments later we both stepped into the scullery, shielding our eyes, until they became accustomed to the brightness of the sunlight.

I could hear the clatter of crockery accompanied by humming. Someone was apparently busy working in the room adjoining the scullery. Hugo quickly put a finger to his mouth, motioning me to keep quiet whilst tip-toeing into the kitchen, where Mrs Burgess, who had her back towards us, was busying herself with some cooking. We crept around the large kitchen table, where we had earlier enjoyed her cake and made our way silently towards the door, when she suddenly turned around and saw us.

'Oh... goodness me, you near frightened me to death!' she gasped, clutching her chest in a slightly melodramatic manner. 'I didn't hear you two come in.'

'Sorry Mrs B, we just popped in for a drink – I think Suzann is finding the tour thirsty work.' He winked at me conspiratorially.

Not wanting to lie deliberately, I decided not to say anything, as Mrs B poured some juice.

Ten minutes later, when I had finished my drink and calmed down considerably from our excursion under the house, we continued our tour, but this time of the upstairs rooms. The house reminded me of a stately home Mum had taken me to visit one holiday. I recalled being a bit disappointed, not by the grandeur or style of the house, which was beautiful, but because we only saw a fraction of it. It had forty-two bedrooms, but we were only allowed to see four of them. Rope barriers barred entry to interesting corridors and doors marked 'Private' were everywhere, and, of course, I wanted to see what lay behind them. My present guide, however, was only too pleased to show me as much as I wanted to see – no doors were off-limits. Hugo spoke knowledgably and enthusiastically as he led me from room to room. We stopped, however, outside one particular room, where he turned to me and said: 'Are you afraid of ghosts?' Carefully, he scanned my face for any tell-tale sign that I might be.

'No,' I answered, returning his gaze. 'Are you?'

'Of course not, especially living here. We have loads of ghosts and strange goings on, I can tell you.

'This room,' Hugo announced as he opened the door to reveal a large wood-panelled bedroom, 'is Lady Carlotta's room and is one of the most haunted rooms in the house.'

Is it? I thought to myself, as I wandered in and quickly scanned the room, which was dominated by a high four-poster bed. The wooden posts were ornately carved and draped with velvet curtains of a dark burgundy colour. This colour was repeated around the room, in the bed cover, curtains and the window seat cushions. The other furniture was of the same mahogany finish as the bed, which gave the impression of unity. It must have been a lovely room at one time, although now it was very much past its prime. Sections of the velvet were faded and frayed by time and the sun, and dust clung to the fabric like a transparent veil.

Hugo was still in his 'tour guide' mode and was providing me with some dates of some of the furniture and paintings within the room, but, to be honest, I was only half listening. I was examining a number of framed miniature portraits which were arranged on top of a large chest of drawers, when something caught my eye in the mirror above. The reflection of the room was somewhat distorted as the mirror was obviously ancient and showed patches of metal and rust on the surface of the glass. However, as I peered into it, I could see that Hugo and I were not alone, for seated on the window seat was a pretty young girl, probably in her early teens, dressed in a pale lilac dress which flowed to her feet. Her dark hair was piled on top of her head except for a few carefully selected curls at the side. She was looking directly at me, with a faint smile of recognition etched across her face. I turned quickly to look back at the room and the window seat was empty. Looking back in the mirror, the reflection revealed an empty space where I had seen her sitting.

'What do you think then?' Hugo was asking me.

'About what?'

'You haven't been listening, have you? I've been telling you about my ancestor who is supposed to haunt this part of the house and you are not interested.'

'Oh I am!' I said, slightly embarrassed. 'Really I am, I was just admiring the lovely room and these pictures. Please tell me about the young lady who haunts this room.'

'I never said she was a young lady.'

'I thought you did.' I was feeling a bit awkward now and aware that Hugo was looking at me a little intensely.

'This is Lady Carlotta's bedroom. She was my great grandmother.'

'What happened to her?'

'I'm not too sure, people say that she died of a broken heart.'

'What did she look like?' I asked before I realised how ridiculous that sounded. How would he know what his great grandmother looked like? But I wanted to know if the image I had seen in the mirror was that of Lady Carlotta.

Thankfully, Hugo didn't flinch at being asked this question, and told me that there was a picture of her at the top of the main staircase and he would show it to me later.

Hugo's tireless enthusiasm for his home seemed endless, as we continued with the tour. I lost count of the number of rooms we went into; there were even rooms within rooms. Not many bathrooms, though, but what a great place to play hide-and-seek!

Eventually, Hugo announced that his tour was complete and that he was now 'starving', so it must be lunch time and we made our way back towards the kitchen, via the galleried landing. We stopped abruptly in front of one of the many portraits which lined the long wall.

'This... is Lady Carlotta. She was quite a beauty in her day.'

I turned to see a woman, possibly in her twenties, with dark hair, which hung down in ringlets. Her big brown eyes looked down at me; I knew instantly that it was the same person I had seen earlier, although she was a few years younger than she was shown to be in the portrait. She certainly looked beautiful in a cream lace dress. So I knew at least who it was I had seen, all I now needed to know was what did she want of me? I thought to myself, as we made our way towards the kitchen, from where a lovely smell was radiating.

*

After lunch, which consisted of Mrs B's homemade soup followed by cheese and pickle sandwiches, Hugo suggested we go for a gentle ride and he would show me the grounds, but not before he let me see the kittens again.

In the stables, we found the kittens in a playful mood. Their mother kept a watchful eye whilst I stroked them. I couldn't resist picking up the ginger one who purred softly as I cuddled her, but only for a few moments as I could tell Hugo was keen to get going. He reintroduced me to my ride, the beautiful chestnut mare I had seen on my previous visit, called 'Flame', who, I couldn't help noticing, was larger than any horse I had ridden before.

Hugo helped me to saddle up and, thankfully, rather than giving me a 'leg-up', he led Flame into the courtyard and up to a much-worn mounting block. He held the reins whilst I managed to get myself seated and I hoped I could remain so for the duration of the ride, and at the same time, that my mare's name didn't indicate a fiery temperament!

It was easy to spot the more experienced of the two of us before we had even left the stable block, as Hugo mounted with confident elegance.

'Are you OK?'

'Yes, fine,' I replied, trying to sound convincing.

'Don't worry, I won't go fast – promise,' Hugo said with a slightly mischievous smile etched across his face.

Please, don't let me embarrass myself, I thought to myself, as we set off at a gentle pace towards the rear of the Manor. We then took a route across a field and down a bridle path up onto Holborn Chase, with its mellow contours dotted with distinctive ancient barrows. It looked beautiful, especially so with the added height advantage. Hugo was true to his word and didn't go fast, asking me if I wanted to canter and then gallop, before actually doing so. I began to relax and actually enjoy the ride. The afternoon was warm and the sun was breaking through some light fluffy clouds, which cast a few shadows on the fields of wheat and barley as we galloped past, exhilarating stuff! I don't remember my riding lessons being quite like this.

After a while, we slowed to a walk as we made our way down a bridle path overhung with trees and Hugo told me a little about his life at the Manor, his family and school. He didn't seem to enjoy school much from what he said; he preferred being at home. Mind you, given a choice, I suppose being at home is where most kids would rather be. His friends don't live near to him and so he did not get to see them much during the holidays. I guess he must get pretty bored in the long school holidays.

He told me something of his father's struggle to keep the Manor going.

'It costs heaps to run the Manor, there's always something which needs mending or replacing. The roof needs patching up at the moment, but we can't just pop down to the local DIY store and buy what we need. The place is listed, so we have to get them specially made which costs a whole lot more. That's just one of hundreds of jobs which need doing. Father is trying his best to get the place sorted so we can get visitors in, or else... well I daren't contemplate what might happen. Anyway, Father has some plans to market the place which means we have then got some money to spend doing the place up. Shall we turn back now?'

We turned, quickened our pace, and cantered most of the way back, which I really enjoyed. We took the same route back and very soon the back of the house loomed into view. I was hoping that Phil was still around and hadn't gone back without me, so I was quickly scanning the rear of the house and grounds for any sign of him, when I caught sight of one of the windows on the first floor and I know that I wasn't mistaken, but there was a shadow at the window.

'Which is Lady Carlotta's bedroom window?' I asked nonchalantly.

'The double one in the centre. Why?'

'Oh, just wondered.'

Hugo turned to look at me quizzically and opened his mouth as if he were going to say something but, deciding against it, turned and headed for the stable block, where Phil was talking to Hugo's father.

'Ah, there you are,' Hugo's father said. 'We had almost given you up for lost. Had a good ride have you, jolly good?' He took hold of my reins to gently bring Flame to a stop and then helped me dismount.

I thanked Hugo and his father for inviting me.

'Why don't you come over later in the week?' Hugo said, whilst effortlessly sliding off his saddle.

'Yes, why don't you? Pop over with Phil on Thursday. It's good for Hugo to have some friends from the village.'

'OK. Thank you, I'd like that.' And I really meant it.

*

'So, how did you get on?' Phil asked as we drove home.

'Well I didn't get on the horse very well – I needed the mounting block!' I joked. 'But I didn't fall off, thank goodness. Although tell that to my legs, they already feel stiff, I'm sure I will ache tomorrow as much as if I had fallen off! But it was good fun.'

'What did you think of Hugo then?'

'Yeah, he seemed OK.'

'I think his dad's a bit concerned about the amount of time he spends on his own, especially in the holidays, because none of his friends live round here. From what I've seen of him, he seems nice enough.'

'Mmm,' was all I managed to say in reply, as I hadn't quite made up my mind about him yet, remembering the episode in the secret passage.

'Nice place though, don't you think?'

'Yes, amazing,' I said, thinking about all those

wonderful rooms we had visited and, as we lapsed into silence, broken only by Phil's characteristic tuneless whistling, I wondered about the young Lady Carlotta I had seen. It had certainly been an interesting day, that's for sure.

FOUR

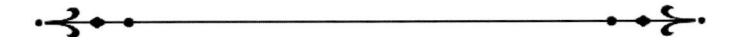

The next morning, bright and early, Alicia arrived like a ray of sunshine, her short blonde curls bobbing as she burst into the house, allowing the warmth of her energy to radiate the place immediately. It didn't take the girls long to sort out what they were going to take with them for their day out so they were soon on their way to Durley Manor.

In Megan's car the two girls chatted amiably, when a song popped into Cara's head which she absentmindedly started to hum. Presently, Alicia, recognising the tune joined in and they sang the remainder together until the end, when they both started laughing.

'I think you had better put the radio on, Mum, as it will be better than listening to us.'

Meg had secretly enjoyed listening to them singing

but, did as she was asked and switched on the radio where they were treated to the very same song the girls had just been singing.

'What a coincidence,' Megan remarked as they approached the entrance to the estate.

'Oh, look there's the gatehouse,' Alicia exclaimed as they pulled though the open ornate wrought iron gates. 'How different it seems.'

'You didn't mention that you had been here before, Alicia,' Megan said, peering at her through the rear-view mirror.

'Er… well… I haven't actually been…' Alicia nervously replied as she tried to think of a plausible explanation.

'We read about it in a book,' Cara quickly responded, knowing they were both hopeless liars, it was best to stick close to the truth.

'Oh, I see. Was that at school?'

Meg didn't get a reply to that question, as they were all absorbed by the long avenue of trees flanked by carefully clipped hedges, set in a beautifully landscaped park; and through the gaps was a tantalising quick view of the Manor.

'This all looks a bit different from the description

we read,' Cara whispered to her friend.

They drove a little further, where, after a bend in the drive, the house was finally fully revealed to them. Standing in a sea of manicured lawns, it was, Cara thought, exactly how she had imagined it from Suzann's diary, right down to the ivy growing up part of the walls, although no longer as rampant, it looked to have been tamed by careful pruning.

After the car had been parked in the visitor car park, they made their way to a building to the right of the Manor, following signs for 'Entrance'.

'I think this must be the old stable block,' Cara mentioned, recognising it from the description given by Suzann.

'I think you are probably right,' her mother replied, admiring her daughter's powers of deduction.

The old stables had been converted into a visitor centre which now held the ticket office, toilets, shop and café. A reminder of its former use, Cara could see in the café where a few cobbled stalls had been left, providing partitioned alcoves for a few tables and chairs. Once their tickets had been bought, they were told that if they were quick, they could make the next guided tour of the house.

Their house guide was a woman who looked to be

in her mid-fifties who couldn't have been more excited and proud to show people around if she tried; her enthusiasm was difficult to conceal. After the usual 'Health and Safety' talk as well as what she described as 'House Rules':

'Please do not sit on, or touch items in the house or deviate from our tour, as we must remember that although this may look like a museum, it is still someone's home. Please feel free to ask as many questions as you like as we go around and I will do my best to answer them.'

The tour commenced, starting in the vast main hall with its armaments and exposed timbers. Here, both Cara and Alicia were pleased to notice that it matched Suzann's account perfectly as if nothing seemed to have changed. Their tour guide was giving a potted history of the house, pointing up at various portraits when certain names were mentioned, which the girls found a bit boring. They were still a bit fed up that she had only got as far as the 1820s by the time they were led out of the hall via the library to the study; here though, the girls started to pay more attention to what was being said, expecting to hear mention of the secret passageway. Their guide, however, continued her monologue about furniture, pictures and their respective artists, before going on to talk about a few rare books and who had acquired them. Cara's patience had worn thin by this stage.

'Excuse me but, isn't there supposed to be a secret passageway in here?'

Their enthusiastic guide, who had hardly stopped to draw breath since the start of their tour, seemed momentarily disappointed at the interruption.

'I am sorry my dear,' she replied, quickly recovering her composure, 'but I'm afraid not.'

'I thought I read somewhere that it was behind that bookcase,' Cara continued undeterred, pointing at the bookcase next to the fireplace.

'I suppose a lot of old houses like this had secret passageways at one time but I don't know of one here,' the guide answered, looking slightly sad that she hadn't been able to provide one for her visitor. 'Shall we continue? If you would like to follow me…'

Cara could feel herself blushing, feeling a little stupid now for asking the question. But she couldn't help thinking that Suzann was right about the description of the house, why should she be wrong about the passageway?

They trailed after their leader, in and out of a few more rooms, before she led them to the first floor via a back staircase by which time the family history was up to the 20th century, so the girls listened keenly for snippets of information that would tie in with Suzann, especially when one of the group decided to ask about the present owner.

'Oh well…' Once again she seemed a bit disorientated at the interruption to her script, as she hadn't quite reached that stage in the family history. 'Lord Easton is the current owner, he inherited from his father twenty-four years ago.'

'So he lives here, does he?' an elderly lady behind Cara asked.

'Well yes, he does some of the time but he has other properties he divides his time between.'

'Alright for some,' A man at the back remarked.

'Right then,' she said, sounding slightly uncomfortable. 'Shall we continue?'

Cara and Alicia were both disappointed to be shown only four of the now seventeen bedrooms. Cara thought they must have converted some of them to bathrooms as Suzann had said there were twenty-two. The last bedroom they visited looked slightly familiar, thanks to the detailed description in the diary.

'Is this Lady Carlotta's bedroom?' Cara found herself asking before she could stop herself.

'Why, yes it is,' their guide replied, sounding surprised and at the same time delighted at her apparent knowledge.

'Is this the room which is haunted?' Alicia asked, encouraged by her friend's bravery.

This was met by a laugh from their guide who replied that she hadn't heard any reports of it being so. But when she saw the look of disappointment on Alicia's face, added that there had been reports of a few odd bumps in the night in another part of the house.

Soon after that, they were led back to the main hall, where the group dispersed, their tour of the house at an end.

Back in the old stables, whilst Megan was queueing up for their lunch, the girls, having found an empty table, discussed what they had managed to find out from their visit, which they decided wasn't much. They agreed that Suzann must have visited the place at some time as her descriptions were accurate but the lack of a secret passageway and a ghost, they decided, must have been a figment of her active imagination. After being laughed at by the guide, Alicia's interest was already beginning to wane; she strongly suspected it was just a story after all. But Cara wasn't too keen to dismiss it just yet.

They had just finished off their lunch and were waiting for Meg, who had nipped to the loo, when the guide approached their table.

'I am glad I caught you,' she gushed. 'I just wanted to let you know, that I asked the senior guide here if there had been any priest holes or secret passageways ever found in the house, and you were right, there is one in the study but it has been closed up for a long time, as it is not safe. I haven't worked here for all that long and not many people even know it exists. So I wondered, how did you know about it?'

'I read about it somewhere,' Cara simply replied, trying hard to sound convincing.

'Oh, good, well I just wanted to let you know,' she said, and turned and left.

'Well, she was right then,' said Cara, feeling that her initial trust in Suzann had been justified.

'Yeah, that was pretty amazing,' replied Alicia.

'But not a word to Mum, ok?'

*

Later that day, after Alicia had gone home, Cara decided to do some research. It wasn't difficult to find, as there were lots of links to Durley Manor and Lord Easton. The images of the previous Lord of the Manor, Hugo's father, gave Cara goose bumps, as he was just as Suzann had described complete with a big handlebar moustache and looking every bit the country squire. Hugo, looked to be a rather serious man, as in all the images he wasn't smiling. In his younger days, Cara thought him quite good looking; even in the most recent pictures, he looked like he had taken care of himself, despite the grey hair. Reading his biography confirmed what Suzann had said, that he was an only child, his mother having died when he was young. She calculated that he was now fifty-eight. There was nothing else she could see of any great relevance.

Reflecting on their day trip, Cara decided that it had been very useful, as they had found out a few things which confirmed Suzann hadn't been making it all up. They now knew that she most definitely had visited the Manor for the accurate and detailed descriptions she had given. Although it could have been as a day tripper, but Cara doubted this. Also, how would she have known about the secret passageway unless she had actually been down there? Phil could have told her about it, Cara presumed, it was a possibility, but again she discounted it, as being a gardener he wouldn't go into the house much, if at all.

But at least she now had a clearer idea which decade the diaries had been written in, based on the fact that Hugo went to boarding school from age nine to eighteen. Cara didn't feel as though the diaries had been written by an older teenager and, Suzann mentioned that Hugo was a similar age to her. Considering his date of birth, 1957 according to his biography, she estimated that the diaries were probably written in the late 1960s or early 1970s, making her between the ages of nine and thirteen, possibly.

Whilst she was mulling over these possibilities, she heard her mother calling for her to come downstairs. Carefully removing a sleepy Lily from her lap, Cara dutifully did as she was asked and found her mum in the kitchen, talking to a woman she had not seen before. Megan interrupted their visitor to introduce Cara to Eileen Symonds, their next-door neighbour.

Cara's first impression, was of a plump woman who looked to be her sixties, with grey hair, which she had made no attempt to disguise. It soon became apparent to Cara that their visitor liked the sound of her own voice, so much so that she could tell that her mother already had quite an earful already. After a couple of polite remarks about Cara, she reverted back to talking about her own son and daughter, who had long since flown the nest. Before she had paused to draw breath, Cara felt she knew so much about them both that she could probably recognise them in the street.

After what seemed like ages listening to this monologue, Megan managed to interrupt her flow.

'Well it's good of you to come round and it's lovely to meet you, Eileen, but we mustn't keep you and I'm afraid we are expecting a call from my husband very shortly, and we haven't eaten yet.'

Too many reasons given, Mum. Cara thought that they sounded like excuses. But it seemed to do the trick as she started to make her way through to the hall.

'Oh, yes, is that the time?' she said, looking at her watch. 'I had better be off. I just wanted to say hello and apologise for not coming around sooner, only, as I said, I've been to stay with our daughter and—'

Cara felt she couldn't bear to hear any more details about her daughter so interrupted.

'Do you know if the lady who lived here had any children?'

'Mildred? No, she didn't. She was a retired school teacher, never married but she was such a nice person and—'

'So when did you move here?'

'Let me see… it must have been… Ian was fourteen at the time and he's thirty-five now, so that's twenty-one years ago. I remember when—'

'Do you know who lived here before Mildred?' Cara continued.

Despite her desire to be rid of their neighbour, Megan was surprised by her daughter's interruptions.

'Cara, don't be rude,' she said gently. 'Why all the questions?'

'Sorry,' Cara replied, feeling herself blush. 'I am just curious about the history of the house, that's all.'

'That's all right.' Eileen appeared not to be offended in the slightest, leaving Megan to think that this sort of thing must happen quite often.

'If you are interested in history, you should speak to Clive, my husband. He loves history and he is from around here. Anyway, I had better be off.'

'Nice to meet you,' Megan said before she closed the door. 'She's a bit of a talker, isn't she?' she added, raising her eyes to the ceiling for added emphasis. 'And, just as I thought she was on her way, you start asking questions. What's all that about?'

'Just curious,' Cara repeated, turning away slightly to avoid looking at her mum as she would be able to tell that Cara was hiding something. 'Because I have never lived in an old house, I am interested to know a bit about its history and who has lived here before.' Which was partly true, Cara thought to herself.

Megan took this to be a positive sign that her daughter was beginning to settle into their new home, so didn't wish to discourage any activity which helped that process.

'Well, perhaps you should take up Eileen's offer and speak to her husband.'

'Yes, I think I might,' Cara replied. 'What time did you say Dad is calling?'

'Sorry darling,' Megan said, feeling guilty. 'He's not. It was the first excuse that came into my head. I know she means well but, she did go on a bit.'

Seeing the disappointment on her Cara's face, Meg reached over to hug her daughter and whispered: 'I know he will ring when he can. I'm sure he will ring soon.'

Later that night, Cara found she wasn't tired and her thoughts drifted to her dad, wondering when he might ring again, and to stop that now familiar knot of worry from growing, as it usually did when he was away, she decided to distract her thoughts and read a bit more of Suzann's diary.

25 July

Mum had slipped out early this morning – I didn't even hear her go. It was her day at Dr Fitzgerald's house. I remembered, before allowing myself to snuggle down under the cosy confines of the blankets, that I had promised to go riding with Hugo. Quickly dressing in a pair of jeans and a reasonably new T-shirt, I attacked my hair, armed with a sturdy brush and some lotion, which promised to tame and sculpt my wild locks into some sleek salon style, but failed miserably. In the end, I hadn't time to bother with it and, after a bit if a battle, I gave in and scraped it into a pony tail.

After a quick drink, but no time for any breakfast, as Phil hates being late for anything, we were on our way.

When we arrived, twenty minutes later, Hugo was already in the stable block; both horses had been saddled and were ready to go. I felt a bit embarrassed because we were late and he had been waiting.

After a quick few words with Phil about what time to meet up, I glanced over towards Hugo and noticed that he had already mounted his horse, he was obviously in a rush to get going. This meant that I had to mount by myself and without the aid of the mounting block. Thinking very carefully about the correct way to do this whilst, at the same time, aware that I could make a complete fool of myself at any moment, I managed to place my left foot in the stirrup, grab hold of the reins and summoning all my strength, hop a couple of times on my right leg, until I felt I had sufficient 'spring' to propel myself upwards. I miscalculated and caught a glimpse of exasperation on Hugo's face as I bobbed down again for another attempt which, again, was unsuccessful.

At this point, Hugo reached for my reins, saying, 'Stop!' He then led me over to the ancient mounting block, where he silently held on to Flame whilst I got into the saddle, aware that it wasn't just the colour of my hair that must surely resemble my horse's name.

He led the way towards a track at the back of the stable block, followed by the dogs which I learnt were called Hector and Paris. He quickened his pace and the dogs followed us almost to the end of the path but seemed to tire as we broke into a gallop across green fields. Soon it was me who found it difficult to keep up, my gloveless hands were hurting where the stiff reins were biting into my skin, my hair had escaped its flimsy hair band and was whipping my face and getting into my eyes, but I dared not let go my tight hold. Hugo must have sensed that I was some distance behind him as, thankfully, he suddenly drew to an abrupt stop and he waited for me to catch up.

'Do you have to go quite so fast?' I said breathlessly, feeling decidedly cheesed off by now.

'Sorry, you ride so well that I keep forgetting it is a while since you have ridden.'

It's difficult to get cross when someone pays you a compliment.

'There is something I want to show you and I promise I won't go fast.'

Hugo led the way towards a wooded area at the far side of the field. We followed a bridle path, which was overgrown with nettles and other weeds; some were so tall that they brushed against my legs as we made our way deeper into the wood. Swarms of midges hovered under the shady branches like misty lampshades which we tried to avoid. Other insects seemed to 'home in' on us and the horses, no doubt regarding us with carnivorous intentions. One of the joys of riding in the countryside in summer, to literally provide 'eating on the hoof' opportunities for hungry insects!

The wood seemed to be getting denser the further we went, the path looked to have almost disappeared. I thought it would have been virtually impassable but Hugo seemed to know where he was going. *Why does he appear to like dark, dingy places?* I thought to myself. *And why does he like taking me with him?*

Suddenly, without warning, we emerged, to my relief, onto a clear stretch of ground filled with warm sunshine. Looming out of the long grass, in front of us, rose a huge tower which must have stood about seventy feet high. As we circled the tower, I could see that it was not round as it first appeared, but hexagonal in shape. There were a number of small windows dotted along its height at irregular intervals; though the lower ones were boarded up. The top floor appeared to jut out above the lower floors and it was capped by a conical roof which looked more or less in good repair. Hugo dismounted and held Flame for me whilst I did the same. After we had tied our horses' reins to a nearby branch, he made his way to a large wooden door at the base of the tower, where he used some force to open the unlocked door.

So, yet again, it seems, I find myself with Hugo in another dark, damp place. The first thing I was aware of was the smell – like moist peat. It reminded me a bit of Phil's compost heap at the bottom of our garden. Although the door was still open, the room was a bit gloomy as the windows were boarded. The walls were largely of brick, but parts still retained patches of plaster painted an indescribable colour, faded by time and neglect. The floor beneath our feet was paved with stone slabs. In the corners, piled up against the walls, fallen leaves, blown in from outside, gathered together in pyramid-shaped piles, as though someone had deliberately swept them there. The only feature in the room was a plain stone fireplace. The mantelpiece above was broken at one side and leaned slightly as a result; otherwise the room was bare. As it was quite dark, I hadn't noticed a wooden door to the left of the entrance, Hugo managed to open this with comparative ease, and held it open for me. Sometimes manners can be a bit of a pain. I would have felt a bit happier if he had led the way. After all, he, presumably knew where he was going and more importantly, what lay beyond.

Behind the door was a steep spiral staircase,

where the air felt cool compared to the heat of the day outside.

'Where does this go?' I asked before I committed myself to a long climb.

'There are some amazing views from the top. Go on, it's quite safe.'

Feeling only slightly more reassured, I started my ascent. The steps were worn in parts, and there was no hand rail, so I had to steady myself by holding on to the walls. The good thing was that there was some light from windows as we climbed higher, so at least I could see where I was going. Before long we had arrived at a small landing with a couple of doors leading off, one of which was half open. Peering in, I could see a room about half the size of the one downstairs but in a similar state of disrepair.

'This used to be an observation tower when they used to hunt here. They used to have hunting parties, and those who were not taking part in the hunt, would watch from the room at the top,' Hugo told me as we continued our climb.

We passed small windows, and through the decades of grime I could make out the tops of trees but I didn't get the opportunity to linger as Hugo urged me not to look, as it would spoil the effect when we reached the top. After another two landings we reached our destination. It was worth the climb, when we reached the top. A door opened onto a room which was quite large and light due to windows set into each of the walls. Some of the glass was broken or cracked in places but the rest was in remarkably good condition, considering its age and the general overall neglect of the lower part of the building. Hugo was right about the view; it was truly spectacular, with a 360-degree panorama from the windows. You could see for miles in every direction. The tops of houses in the village were visible in one direction; through another window I could see above the tops of trees across the rolling hills and fields, dotted with rural buildings which stretched ahead towards the horizon like a patchwork quilt. Hugo pointed out the Manor from another window, its immense size reduced to that of a miniature dolls' house set amidst a small sea of green. We stood in silence as we took in this fantastic view. It wasn't hard to imagine people here hundreds of years ago doing the same, only they would have been surveying a very different scene, of men on horses chasing after deer and possibly wild boar, while the women looked on from the safety of the tower.

I was still admiring the sight from one of the windows, so I hadn't noticed Hugo leave the room. When I turned around and realised he had gone I decided to make my way down the spiral staircase to find him. When I got to the first landing I noticed a door which was slightly ajar, that I hadn't seen on our way up. Pushing it gingerly, I peered in, gently calling Hugo's name as I did so. There was no immediate response, so I pushed the door open further and stepped inside.

The room was, in contrast to the observation room above, rather dark; the one window looked to have been covered over or partially boarded, so it took a few moments for my eyes to adjust; when they had, I could see that the room contained some furniture of sorts. In front of a stone fireplace, stood a large chair, although it was difficult to see it properly as it was placed with its back towards me. A table stood against one of the walls and was covered with something which I couldn't quite see, so I decided to go and have a closer look. As I got nearer, it became apparent that the table was littered with an assortment of personal items, papers, a cup and a plate, which looked like it had been used recently, as there were remnants of food on it. There also were a couple of old photographs lying on top of various newspapers.

'Don't you touch that!' a gruff male voice commanded. How my heart didn't stop beating there and then I will never know. Instantly dropping the photographs, I spun around to see the figure of a man silhouetted against the veiled light of the window. He was making his way towards me.

I felt almost paralysed with fear; I was unable to move from the spot, my eyes were fixed on the tall shape of this man who was dressed in a dirty-looking tweed jacket, tied in the middle with some string. Even in this dim light I could see that his trousers were equally grubby and had a large hole in one knee. The most alarming thing about him was his eyes; they were a piercing light grey, in contrast to the rest of his face, which was dark due to it being partially concealed by a beard. His eyes seemed to hold me hypnotised. As he got closer the strong odour of alcohol and sweat mixed with a musty smell associated with old things met my nostrils, I also had a sense of something else but I didn't have time to make sense of it, as my temporary paralysis subsided and I let out a scream and headed for the door as fast as my quivering legs would take me and down the precarious stairway. I could hear his heavy footsteps behind me as I lurched into the ground floor room, very nearly colliding with Hugo, closely followed by the strange looking man.

'There's a man,' I managed to stammer breathlessly, clutching at Hugo's arm.

'It's alright, Suzann,' Hugo said, remarkably calmly, and addressed the figure that had now appeared at the stairway door. 'What are you doing here, Todd? You know my father doesn't like you staying here; the building isn't safe, you know that.'

'I know, Master Hugo, but I just like to keep my eye on the place. Sorry, I didn't mean to scare the young girl.'

'Well, don't let my father catch sight of you here.'

'Alright, Master Hugo,' Todd replied meekly.

'I think we had better be going,' Hugo said, looking down at my fist still clamped onto his sleeve.

I immediately released my grip, and headed for the door, relieved to be getting out into the fresh air. Once outside, I leaned against the wall of the tower as my legs were still shaking, then Hugo emerged.

'You could have told me you were going downstairs,' I raged. 'I didn't know he was there.'

'Neither did I. He's quite harmless. He does a few odd jobs around the place. My father turns a blind eye to him sleeping in a few of our unused buildings, but he doesn't like him in here, because it's not too safe.'

'You didn't tell *me* it wasn't safe!' I said, feeling now slightly cross.

'Oh, don't worry, it's not falling down, it's just that it isn't safe to live in.'

'Who is he?'

'His name is Todd Rowland, he grew up here. His father and grandfather both used to work here many years ago.'

'Do you know what happened to him to end up like this?'

'Not really. All I know is that my grandfather had to sell off some land years ago, together with a number of farms, which included the one that Todd's father rented. I believe the family had to move away to find other work. That's all I know, except that a few years ago, Todd reappeared. Father took pity on him, and gave him work when he could. Shall we make our way back? I am starving.'

Hugo helped me to mount Flame and we made our way back to the Manor where Mrs B had lunch ready and waiting for us. Even though I had missed breakfast, I hadn't realised just how hungry I was. Thankfully Hugo had a good appetite and didn't seem to notice me tucking in to the selection of sandwiches laid out for us on the kitchen table, together with some homemade scones and jam. I couldn't help but wonder whether Hugo received this kind of treatment every day.

*

After lunch, Hugo suggested we go for a walk, as he had something else he wanted to show me. I was secretly hoping it wasn't yet another attempt to frighten me to death in some dark, dank place. Thankfully, he suggested that we walk, which I was really glad about, as my body still hadn't got used to riding yet. In fact, I could feel my legs starting to stiffen up and my hands were still a bit sore.

Hugo led me towards the back of the house and down a path until we reached a five-bar gate, which he opened and let me through. To our left we came across a large impressive stone barn. Immediately to the right of it was a section cordoned off by high wire fencing. In the middle of this fence was a wire-covered door, so you could see through quite easily.

Contained within were hundreds of brown-coloured birds, flecked with patches of black. Before I could ask, Hugo told me that they were Red Grouse. His father had been rearing them ready for 'The Glorious Twelfth'.

'What do you mean?'

'The twelfth of August is the start of the shooting season, you numbskull.'

'Oh!'

'My father has organised a shooting weekend. People will pay a lot of money to shoot on our estate and we are providing a weekend package. It should be good.'

'Why are they all caged up like this?'

'We have reared them since the spring but we will be letting them out today, hopefully, although we will still continue to feed them.'

I couldn't help feeling sad – they looked quite delicate, pretty birds. Hugo then proceeded to give me all sorts of information about them but I didn't want to hear any more.

'I think it is time I should be getting back,' I said, glancing at my watch. 'I don't want to keep Phil waiting.'

We walked back in relative silence. When we arrived at the stable block, where I had arranged to meet Phil, he hadn't arrived, so Hugo took me to see the kittens and that cheered me up a bit. They were lively and had managed to break free of their cardboard box. Two were playing together but the one I liked was sat on its own, a little apart from the others, so I scooped it up and cuddled it and, as I stroked its soft fur, I could hear it purr gently.

'Did you ask your mother if you could have one of the kittens?'

'Not yet,' I said, as I had been waiting to catch her in the right mood.

'Better be quick, as one of Mrs B's friends is interested in a couple of them. Don't worry,' he added as he saw the look of disappointment on my face. 'I told her that one is reserved, although I can only do it for a few days.'

'Thanks. I will ask her tonight.'

'I thought I might find you in here.' Looking up, I saw Phil standing in the doorway. It was time to go.

'Come around next week if you like,' Hugo said as I climbed into Phil's car, taking care not to step on a few discarded plant pots which were on the floor.

'OK,' I replied, waving goodbye.

FIVE

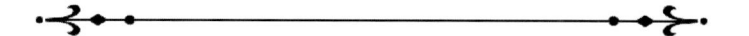

The next day, Cara checked for messages from her father but, there were none. Thankfully, she didn't have much time to dwell on things as she had promised to help her mum in the garden, then later, she was going over to Alicia's for a sleepover.

Just before she went downstairs, she stood looking out of her bedroom window, sighing at the thought of all that work which would be required to transform their messy patch into anything like Eileen and Clive's garden next door, with its abundant flower borders, neatly clipped shrubs and lush green lawn. One of them clearly enjoyed gardening, Cara decided. In fact, she could just make out either Eileen or Clive working at the back of one of the borders and she watched them for a few moments as they bobbed up and down, weaving between the tall shrubs, as they were partially visible one second, the next obscured by bushy vegetation, making it difficult to see which one of them it was. Cara continued to look, as she was interested to see what Clive looked like. A few moments later her patience was rewarded with a glimpse of what was clearly a woman, wearing a cardigan and a skirt bending over some flowers. The funny thing was, that this woman didn't look anything like Eileen, as she looked older, had curly grey hair and was much slimmer than Eileen. Puzzled, Cara watched until this lady once again became enveloped by the tall plants and disappeared from view. Cara kept up her vigil, hoping she would re-emerge, until she heard her mother calling for her and she went downstairs.

Even though mother and daughter spent most of the day outside, Cara didn't see anyone in next door's garden, nor was there any sign that anyone was at home. Despite the warm temperatures, all the windows were closed. Cara decided that they must have some help with the garden and made a mental note to ask Eileen when she popped around to speak to her husband.

*

Alicia's sleepovers were always great fun. She was a popular girl at school and an invitation to one was highly sought after amongst her wide circle of friends. The popularity of this event was not diminished by the fact of her having two older twin brothers, Elliot and Oliver, who were considered to be very good looking by most of the female population at school and their presence in the rugby team did much to swell the number of supporters at home matches. Despite their looks and physique, both boys remained down to earth and level headed, which in turn merely increased their appeal. So while the sight of these two hunks could render many an intelligent, articulate girl to one with a latent speech impediment, Cara remained unaffected; having grown up with them, she treated them both like the brothers she never had.

Alicia's family home was outside of the small village of Fordingham, surrounded by fields of ripening wheat and barley. The house was large and old; having originally been a farm house, it had been sympathetically renovated by Alicia's parents into a modern, spacious home, which Cara loved.

Like most of the rooms in the house, Alicia's was large and square and overlooked the back garden. It was decorated in a typically feminine way, in gentle blues, pinks and creams, colours Alicia often liked to wear, so it suited her personality well. On the floor, large cushions had been placed together with some bean bags and a few mattresses had been propped up against a wall for them to use later for sleeping, not that much of that ever happened at Alicia's sleepovers.

The girls, Florence, Isabella, Rose and Georgina, arrived shortly after Cara, already wearing their pyjamas, and quickly settled themselves down on the cushions and bean bags to exchange holiday news and gossip, nibbling on various snacks which Alicia's mum had brought in for them and laid out on a couple of trays on the floor, around which the small group had arranged themselves, as though they were sitting around a campfire.

Isabella, or Bella as she was called by her friends, decided she wanted to tell the girls about a story she heard recently and suggested they dim the lights to create the 'right atmosphere'.

'Well,' she said, once the lights were dimmed, and had paused for dramatic effect to make sure she had their full attention before continuing, 'are you sitting comfortably? Then I will begin… Remember, what I am about to tell you is a true story.'

Isabella then started to recount her tale about a man who was driving along a motorway with three friends as passengers. Behind, was another car containing another member of their party. All was well for most of the journey until the two cars became separated on a particularly busy stretch of the motorway. The second car eventually caught up with the first car, only to see that it had pulled over onto the hard shoulder. On closer inspection it looked as though it had been involved in an accident. The driver of the second car pulled over a short distance behind the first car, anxious to see if they were alright. Thankfully, he noticed the two passengers were already standing to one side looking shaken but, otherwise unhurt. The driver of the first car could be seen slowly emerging from the open door but, before long appeared to be talking to someone unseen quite agitatedly, as though arguing. Suddenly he stopped protesting and his body slumped as though admitting defeat, he then walked to the front of the car and disappeared from view.

The driver of the second car, having seen all this went to join his friends huddled together besides their car, to find them all very distraught. Looking into the damaged car he saw his friend, the driver, dead at the wheel.

'So who was it they saw outside the car arguing?' Florence asked, not sure she had understood.

'The driver of the first car of course,' Isabella

replied. 'It's his ghost arguing with whoever has come to take him to heaven, that he didn't want to go.'

The other four girls seemed stunned into silence.

'Honestly it's as true as I sit here,' Isabella announced.

'I'm not sure I believe in ghosts,' Florence said quietly.

'That's because you've probably never seen or heard one,' replied Isabella authoritatively.

'And you have?' Alicia enquired.

'Well, I haven't seen one exactly but, I've heard one, or at least my sister has,' Isabella replied less confidently.

'You do hear stories, don't you?' Alicia continued, looking knowingly at Cara. 'And wonder whether they are real or not.'

'Well, I heard a rather strange story…' Rose said, and went on to tell of odd goings on at her aunt's house one Christmas.

So an hour or two passed telling of ghosts and strange happenings, each one becoming more frightening and perhaps a little bit more absurd than the last, as though in competition with one another for the scariest story. In the midst of one of these, they heard an unusual noise, which the girls tried at first to ignore, until it was too loud to dismiss. It sounded like a scratching noise emanating from the wall. They all stopped talking, and looked around anxiously at each other, when they saw Alicia's bedroom door open very slowly, followed by a large hairy hand with huge talons. Georgina screamed loudly just as a white figure appeared, covered from head to foot in flowing veils. The rest of the girls joined in the screams with the exception of Alicia and Cara.

'Elliot, if you are going to dress up as a ghost in an old sheet, you could at least have taken your trainers off,' Alicia retorted.

Oliver followed brandishing the hairy hand, which he proceeded to dangle in front of his sister without a satisfactory reaction.

'What you up to then?' Elliot enquired, taking off the sheet and sitting down next to Rose, who did not seem unhappy to have him there, unlike his sister.

'We're telling ghost stories,' Rose replied. 'Do you know any?'

'Nah, don't like stories,' Elliot stated, deciding that gate crashing his sister's sleepover wasn't as much fun as he thought.

'I prefer to talk to some real ghosts.'

'What do you mean?' asked Georgina.

'You mean to tell me you have never used a Ouija board before?' Oliver asked, joining in.

The girls all looked at each other blankly.

'What is it?' Florence asked.

'It's where you have letters of the alphabet arranged around a glass and you all put your fingers on it and ask questions, then the glass moves and spells out an answer,' Elliot explained.

'Oooo, let's have a go, shall we?' Isabella said, eyes wide with excitement. 'What do we need?'

Soon the boys were organising the girls and before long they were sat around an upturned tray with the letters arranged around a glass in the centre. Elliot got up to join his brother who dimmed the lights.

'Aren't you two staying?' Rose asked, unable to hide her disappointment.

'Nah, we need our beauty sleep. Sweet dreams, girls,' Elliot replied on his way out.

'What do we do now?' Rose asked, looking a bit forlorn.

'We ask a question, I suppose,' Isabella replied, determined to continue with it.

'What shall we ask?' Alicia said.

'Who are we talking to?' asked Florence, feeling rather apprehensive.

'Ghosts, of course. Honestly Flo, keep up,' Isabella retorted.

They all put a finger onto the glass, then Isabella asked: 'Is anybody there?'

The glass remained where it was. Rose then repeated the question. Again, the glass did not move. Cara thought this a silly game but didn't want to be the first to say so.

'Is anybody there?' Isabella persisted.

They waited for something to happen.

'This isn't going to work, is it?' Alicia said, beginning to feel a bit bored.

'Just give it a minute. Perhaps if we ask a different question?' Georgina suggested.

'Like what?' Cara enquired.

'Do you have a message for anyone here?' Isabella asked.

They all felt the glass move slowly towards 'Yes'.

'Are you moving it, Bella?' Georgina asked accusingly.

'No, I swear I am not.'

'Shhh,' Rose said. 'Who is your message for?'

The glass moved more confidently now towards C then A then R then A.

'Someone must be moving it,' Cara said, beginning to feel very uncomfortable. They all promised that no one was moving the glass.

'Ask who the message is from?' Alicia suggested.

'Who is the message from?' Isabella asked the board.

The glass moved to an S then U then Z followed by ANN.

Cara immediately removed her finger from the glass and pushed herself away from the group.

'Just stop this. I am not doing this anymore. Someone, Alicia, is moving the glass and it's not funny,' Cara said, looking at her best friend and trying not to show how upset she felt at her friend's betrayal. *How could she?* Cara thought to herself. *And how much has she told the others about Suzann's diaries?* It was supposed to be their secret.

'What do you mean?' Alicia asked, and went over towards Cara who had now removed herself to the other side of the room and was switching on a small lamp.

'I think you know very well what I mean – you were moving the glass!'

'No, honestly Cara I didn't, I wouldn't—'

'Look, I don't think there is any point in continuing this, I'm tired anyway,' Cara said, turning her back on Alicia. She then proceeded to unroll her sleeping bag.

As the others looked on, mystified. Florence asked if anyone had been moving the glass, to which they all replied, 'No.'

'Don't you want to know what the message was?' Georgina enquired.

'No, because someone is just messing about and thinks it's funny, but it's not,' Cara replied looking at Alicia, who just shook her head sadly.

There was a definite chill in the air after that and the mood became sombre as the four girls cleared away the tray of letters, then they too got out their sleeping bags and decided to go to sleep.

Cara remained awake long after she could hear the gentle snores and deep breathing of her companions. She was too upset to sleep as this was the first time the two friends had fallen out. Cara managed to send a text to her mum, asking to be picked up before breakfast the next morning, before she eventually drifted off.

SIX

Cara woke early the next morning, after a poor night's sleep, and crept downstairs quietly so as not to wake the girls, hoping her mum had seen her text. She was both relieved and surprised to see Uncle Ben standing in the hallway talking to Alicia's father. When Ben saw Cara, he immediately turned on his cheerful grin and it was about then that Cara suspected something was going on. They left almost straight away.

'Where's Mum?' Cara asked as soon as they had left the house.

'She's at home, wasn't feeling too good this morning, so she asked me if I could pick you up and as you're my favourite niece, how could I refuse?' He grinned back at her.

'What's the matter with her?'

'Oh, just a bad headache, honestly she's fine.'

Cara wasn't convinced by his performance, nor by the cheerful music blaring from his CD, or his constant chatter. She could feel that something wasn't right.

Uncle Ben let them both into the house and Cara went in search of her mum, who she found standing in the kitchen. She recognised the signs as soon as she saw Meg: the puffy eyes, red nose and tissues stuffed up the sleeve of her cardigan.

'Mum?'

'Do you want me to stay, Meg?' her uncle asked.

Meg merely nodded her reply.

'What's going on, Mum?'

Her mother appeared to have great difficulty trying to do two things at once: maintain her composure whilst speaking, as though the effort involved was just too much, so she simply went over to Cara and held her tightly. Without any words being exchanged, Cara knew something had happened to her father.

It was Uncle Ben who explained to Cara, very gently, what they had been told by the Army officials. That he had been involved in a secret mission to rescue some comrades who were being held captive, however, they had been betrayed. An ambush took place and a number of soldiers had been killed but, Uncle Ben was anxious to stress, her father wasn't one of them; he was classified as 'Missing'.

For Cara, the rest of that day passed as though she were viewing life through a filtered camera lens; nothing seemed real. Various people came and went – officers from the army, she presumed. Aunt Jane arrived and bustled about making endless cups of tea for everyone, which nobody really wanted. Eventually, Cara managed to escape to the solitude of her room, where she found Lily curled up on her bed. She snuggled up next to her, feeling numb.

Sometime later, she heard someone coming up her stairs. Looking up, she saw Alicia, who didn't say anything at first, she just came over and gave Cara a hug.

'I am so sorry, Cara,' she murmured.

It was then that Cara's tears began to flow.

*

Alicia stayed over that night, she wanted to be there for her friend. As always she was kind, thoughtful and understanding. Cara had often envied her ability to instinctively know the right words to say at the right time, in this respect Alicia appeared wiser than her years.

After a breakfast where not much was eaten by anyone, the two disappeared upstairs. It was Alicia who brought up the subject first.

'You have no idea how much trouble Ellie and Ollie are in over that Ouija board. Mum went ballistic with them when she found out. They are grounded for a week. She made me promise never to try it again, as she said you don't know what you are dealing with. She said if you were living in the centre of London you wouldn't put a big sign on your door saying, "Come in, all welcome," would you? Because you would get all sorts of weirdos coming in. She said, that's what Ouija boards are like, they can be dangerous.

'You know I haven't told a single sole about those diaries, don't you?' Alicia continued bravely.

'Yes,' Cara replied, and meant it.

'So do you think it was Suzann trying to contact you?'

'I don't know. But if it was her, I suppose it means she is no longer alive.'

'Not necessarily, as according to my mum, you can get bad spirits coming through pretending to be someone, just to get you hooked. That's one of the reasons why they are dangerous.'

The two remained silent for a few moments, during which Alicia wondered, not for the first time, what the message would have been had they continued.

'Come on, let's read psychic Suzann's diary,' Alicia suggested, partly because she wanted to distract Cara from her worries but also she was still a little intrigued to find out more.

29th July

It's Maud's funeral today. Mum said that I couldn't go. It wasn't 'necessary' for me to attend.

Sometime during the morning, I saw from our front room window that a long black car had arrived. Because there were a few other cars parked immediately outside Maud's house, the hearse pulled up outside our front room window. I watched, through the light drizzle, as two sombre-looking men in matching dark suits got out. Not long after, they returned, wheeling the coffin on a long flat trolley which announced its arrival with a loud squeaking sound, which reminded me of those awful supermarket trolleys which often have at least one dodgy wheel. This undistinguished departure was followed by a small procession of family and friends; Archie was supported by their son and daughter and, following this group, was Maud. She was wearing the same tweed skirt but wore a look of concern which I felt was directed at her husband, but when she passed our window she turned her gaze towards me and smiled. It seemed inappropriate to wave back on such an occasion but I managed a weak smile and hoped no one saw me, especially my mum. What I really wanted to do was shout out to Archie: 'It's OK, Mr Middleton. Maud's fine, she's standing right next to you.' But of course, I couldn't. It's frustrating when no one else can see what I can see.

*

Mum returned just after lunch, looking a little distracted. Following her into the kitchen, I asked how the funeral went.

'Oh, about as well as these things can. Archie wasn't too good, but that's only to be expected. I'll pop around later and see how he is. Pop the kettle on, love, will you?'

I made us a cup of tea and sat down at the kitchen table with her, thinking that this might be a good moment to ask her about the kitten. So I told her all about how lovely they were, stressing that they had to find good homes for them soon. I stressed that I had never before asked for a pet and that cats are quite self-sufficient. Surprisingly she didn't say no, but 'she would think about it'.

Later, when Mum had returned from next door's house, she flopped down on the sofa in the front room. I could see that something was worrying her.

'What's the matter, Mum?'

'Oh, I was just thinking about Archie; it seems he can't find Maud's insurance documents. He's got himself into a bit of a state about it. He's talking about selling the house, if he can't find them, and moving in with his son.'

'Surely there are only so many places Maud could have put them,' Phil said in between mouthfuls of crisps.

'Well, he's had the whole place upside down. I even had a look around this afternoon… I don't know what to suggest.'

'I think he should try the chest of drawers in the attic,' I found myself saying almost as if it was someone else talking.

They both stopped what they were doing and looked at me.

'What do you mean?' Mum asked.

It was no use trying to backtrack, I was committed now. 'The insurance papers, I'm sure Maud mentioned that she had put them there for safe keeping.'

'Why should she tell you that?' Mum looked suspiciously at me.

I merely shrugged my shoulders, and tried not to meet her gaze, as Mum always knows when I am lying.

'I don't know... perhaps I was around at her house one day and she mentioned them... I can't remember, it was a while ago.' I was beginning to feel uncomfortable now, and could feel my face colouring up and I could sense that Mum was about to launch into further interrogation tactics, when the phone in the hall rang. I caught Phil looking quizzically at me, but I quickly averted my eyes and mumbled something about tidying my room and hid there, trying to keep out of Mum's way for the rest of the evening. But, I needn't have worried, Mum spent some time on the phone and when she had finished, she seemed strangely preoccupied and made no further reference to Maud or the insurance papers but, knowing my mother, I knew that she wouldn't forget it.

SEVEN

The next few days passed as though Cara were looking at life through a bit of a haze, as if the sun had partly been obscured from view. Mother and daughter were both going through the motions of everyday life as though in a trance, only to be jolted out of it by the sounds of the phone ringing, bleeping with text messages or if someone knocked at the door. One little ray of sunshine did, however, manage to find its way through to lighten their gloom, in the form of Helen, Megan's mother. She arrived uninvited with an overnight bag and a big heart, having left her husband Bill at home. She immediately assumed command. Not in a bossy, overbearing way, the way some mothers can be but, calmly and efficiently and she met with no resistance from Meg, who was finding it increasingly difficult to function.

So the addition of such a positive force did much to balance out the negative energies in their house. As for Cara, she adored her grandma so was very pleased to see her.

Later, after lunch, leaving Grandma and Mum to catch up, Cara retreated to her quiet attic and sought to lose herself for a while in Suzann's world which, she soon discovered was beginning to mirror her own.

30th July

To my surprise and immense relief, Mum didn't mention Maud the next morning, in fact she didn't say much at all, but when she did, was rather snappier than usual. No one was spared. Phil's boots weren't in the right place and she had 'nearly broken her neck tripping over them', a slight exaggeration, I thought, as I saw her merely step over them muttering something under her breath. Then I 'copped it'; apparently, I was munching my cornflakes too loudly! Thereafter, we had a dumb breakfast. Phil and I looked at each other, as if to say, 'somebody's got out of bed the wrong side this morning', and we kept our heads down.

It wasn't until later, when I was helping clear up after tea that I gained some indication of why Mum had been in such a black mood earlier.

'We will be going up to Yorkshire for a few days next week,' she announced as she briskly dried one of the pans she had vigorously scrubbed a few minutes before.

'Oh... where?' I asked, intrigued.

'York,' Mum said.

'What's there, then?' Honestly, she can be such hard work sometimes.

'My mother.'

Well, that kind of stopped me in my tracks. I can't remember the last time we talked about Granny. It hadn't taken me long to work out that they obviously weren't close, as they never speak on the phone, or visit. When I was younger, I can remember finding some old family photos of Mum when she was young, probably about my age now. She was with a woman and, naturally, I asked questions about who she was, but Mum gave short responses to my questions, making it quite clear that she didn't want to talk about it. So that's why I didn't ask any more about her. Sometimes, privately, I would wonder about her, what she was like and what it would be like to have a grandma, but, 'what you have never had, you never miss', as my mum often says.

I did wonder why now, and asked Mum; all she said was, 'She's ill,' but she said it in such a way that I knew she didn't want to say any more about it. So I didn't, as I knew it wouldn't get me anywhere. However, I did have a lot of questions and I would love to know the answers.

*

Not for the first time did Cara feel slightly amazed by the coincidences contained in Suzann's diary which overlapped her own. Before going on to read the next diary entry, she messaged Alicia and copied her the next few pages. She was just about to start reading again, when she heard the now familiar squeak of the bottom step, warning her that someone was on their way up, so she quickly tucked the diary under her pillow, then moments later Helen appeared and came and sat next to Cara on her bed.

'This is such a lovely room,' she said, glancing around, smiling appreciatively. Until her eyes fell on to the olive carpet, where she raised an eyebrow and added, smiling, 'Well, it will be when you get it all done. What are you up to?'

'Oh, just reading,' Cara replied without thinking.

'And what are you reading?' her grandma enquired, looking around for signs of a book.

'Er… just a book a friend gave me.' Cara never was very good at lying and felt herself blush.

'What's it called?' her grandmother continued to probe.

'Er, I can't remember.' She was feeling very uncomfortable now.

'What's it about then?' Her grandma reminded Cara of a pit bull terrier; she wasn't letting this go. She got the distinct feeling that she knew Cara was hiding something.

'I've only just started really.'

'Well perhaps, when you are ready, you can tell me all about it,' Helen said, getting up and making her way towards the stairs.

'I can see why you would like this room, it has a lovely relaxing feel to it,' Helen added. 'Anyway, I will leave you to your, book.'

And with that she went back downstairs, leaving Cara feeling annoyed with herself at the way she had handled that.

Before Cara resumed her reading, she deliberately

chose a book from her collection, which she had read before, and placed it next to her on the bed, just in case her grandma returned, although she strongly suspected she wouldn't.

3rd August

Today, after breakfast, we left for York. Mum said she had packed some 'provisions' for the journey as it was a long way from Dorset to Yorkshire and she wanted to get there before it got dark as she dislikes driving at night.

Mum wasn't joking about the distance. I kept resisting the temptation to say, 'Are we there yet?' as she was concentrating hard in the heavy traffic on the motorway. A lot of people seemed to have taken advantage of the good weather we had been having and were escaping to various parts of the country, mostly by the M1.

When we eventually reached York we then spent some time getting acquainted with the one-way system as Mum struggled to remember her way around.

'It's all changed since I was here last,' she said, exasperated, as we passed over a bridge for the second time. I wondered just how long ago that was.

The only good thing about getting lost was that it gave me an opportunity to have a look at the city (although why it is called a city, I don't know, as it didn't look all that big to me!). In the fading twilight it looked quite a magical and yet mysterious place. I glimpsed sections of old castellated walls, imposing Georgian buildings and spires reflected in the River Ouse which runs through its centre.

Mum decided eventually to stop and ask someone for directions, then after a short while we turned into a road lined with terraced houses. They were not dissimilar to our own, only these were taller, having another floor, and were painted a creamy white, whilst ours is brick. We pulled up outside a house with number 13 on the dark-painted door. Mum switched off the car engine but didn't move. She just sighed deeply, staring straight in front of her. Was this due to fatigue or relief to have arrived all in one piece, or was it the prospect of the week ahead?

Mum was about to knock on the door of number 13, when the door to the house adjoining it opened and a small woman wearing a bright yellow blouse and a nice smile, made her way over to greet us.

'Oh hello! You must be Maureen and this must be Suzann,' the woman pronounced in a shrill voice that was laced with a Yorkshire accent. 'I am Betty. You must be exhausted, you poor things. Now May's asleep, she had a bad night last night, so we had best not disturb her. But come on in, I've got a key and I've put a casserole in the oven for you.'

She led us into a long, dimly lit hall, with stairs leading off to the left. We passed a couple of doors as we made our way into a room which was part living room, part dining room with an old-fashioned fireplace in the centre of one wall. The rest of the room was cluttered with furniture and ornaments, which made it look smaller than it probably was, although it was difficult to see as this room, like the hall, was poorly lit. However, I wasn't taking much notice as the main object of my attention was the dining table set for two and the appetising smell of food which wafted in our direction, reminding me how hungry I was.

After we had eaten, cleared away and brought our bags in from the car, we quietly made our way upstairs to find our bedrooms. But, it's always the same when you are creeping about, trying not to make too much noise; the opposite happens. The stairs creaked and groaned, Mum banged her bag on the banister and we couldn't find the light switch on the landing. Goodness knows how anyone could sleep through all that commotion. We found our rooms on the second floor, where I quickly changed into my pyjamas and must have fallen asleep as soon as my head touched the soft feather pillow. It's amazing how tired you can get sitting in a car all day doing nothing!

*

Later, that afternoon, Cara went out with her grandma to get a few things they needed from the supermarket. Thankfully, there was no further mention of her choice of reading matter, much to Cara's relief. However, a couple of unusual things occurred, which, had they happened at any other time, she would have completely ignored. The first took place in the car on the way there; she noticed that a car they were following nearly all the way, had her father's initials on the number plate – RGW, Robert Greenwood Wade. The second took place in the 'home baking' aisle, where Cara had been sent to get some baking powder. There were a few women who had stopped for a chat and seemed oblivious to the fact that their trolleys were causing a bit of a blockage in the aisle. As Cara waited to pass them she heard only a fragment of their conversation:

'...Your dad said he is fine, don't worry...'

It made her want to stop and listen to some more, only she couldn't.

In bed that night, Cara wasn't a bit tired and knew she would just lay there and worry about her dad, so she turned once more to Suzann's diary, wondering what, if any other coincidences she might uncover. She wasn't disappointed.

4th August

It felt odd waking up in a strange bed. For a few moments I lay there, unsure of where I was, looking up at an unfamiliar ceiling with its green lace lampshade hanging down from the central ceiling rose. The white cotton sheets smelled like they must have been stored in some cupboard for decades.

Once I had realised where I was, bits of yesterday's journey flitted into my thoughts. Two things in particular; firstly, Mum told me a little about her early life. Being together in the car for all that length of time, it was more difficult for her to escape my questions. She gave me the impression that she wasn't close to her mum, but I had kind of worked that one out for myself, although she didn't say why. Mum's father, Sid, worked on the railway but he died when Mum was quite young. Mum apparently left home when she was sixteen and worked at a local solicitor's office where she met my dad, whom she married when she was eighteen. Dad then got a new job down in Dorset and so they both moved away from York.

The other topic of conversation in the car which I mulled over was of a more positive nature. We somehow got talking about animals. Whether I had skilfully engineered this I can't quite remember but it doesn't really matter, because I told Mum that I would have to let Hugo know whether I wanted the kitten soon otherwise it would go to someone else. I had semi-rehearsed a little speech in my head and the persuasive tactics I would use, including the name I had chosen, Lily, to help win Mum over to the idea, but this was not needed as she said YES!

I sat up in bed and scanned the small room I had slept in. It had the look of a spare room about it. There were a few boxes piled at one end, next to an old wooden wardrobe, which had a mirror set into the door. To the right of it was a matching large chest of drawers, which gleamed with years of careful polishing, but each of the five drawers had different handles. On top of this was a small collection of photographs in an assortment of frames and I got out of bed to have a closer look at them. There were a couple of black and white photos of people grouped together at the seaside, another of a young woman, a man standing in a garden with a little girl who looked a bit like my mother, and some very old sepia photos of stern-looking men and women in old-fashioned clothes.

I heard a noise downstairs and thought Mum was probably up, so I hurriedly got dressed and headed downstairs where I found Mum in the kitchen, making tea.

'How's Granny?' I asked.

'She's fine, I'm just going to take her a cup of tea.'

'Oh, can I do that?'

'No, that's OK. I'll do it – you make yourself some breakfast. There's bread in the bread bin, the butter and juice are in the fridge.' Mum took the cup and saucer and headed for the stairs.

I sat down at the small kitchen table, munching on some toast, and wondered what we were going to be doing all week. Although it was great to be meeting my grandma at long last, there didn't appear to be much that a girl my age could do, especially with Mum probably being housebound, helping Granny. My thoughts drifted back to home and the lovely rides across the Chase on Flame's back, darting over the fields with Hugo close behind, and I just hoped that I wouldn't get too bored.

*

Mum spent quite some time upstairs with Granny that first morning. I was glad I had remembered to bring my book with me but, by eleven thirty, I had nearly finished it and was beginning to worry that I would have nothing else to occupy me for the rest of the day, when Mum appeared and announced that we would be going into York, as she needed to do some food shopping and we could have a look around the centre of town. What a relief!

Apparently Granny was too tired to see me but would hopefully feel better later, Mum told me. We were making our way, in Mum's car, through the dreaded one-way system we had encountered yesterday but, this time, we were a bit more familiar with it.

York city centre wasn't as big as I imagined it to be, but that was no disappointment as you could walk around it in a morning. I loved the little old streets which time seemed to have forgotten. Some of the houses on opposite sides of these streets almost seemed to touch each other as they were tiered, each floor hanging precariously over the one below. Mum and I spent some time browsing in the market square with its cobbled streets, getting a few supplies for Granny. When we had finished, Mum suggested we go and have a look at Clifford's Tower, before a walk on the old walls that almost completely surround this lovely city.

At school, I really quite enjoy history, although many of my friends would disagree, saying it was 'boring'. We have been learning a bit about the Romans and I remember our teacher mentioning that York had been quite a large Roman settlement, so the thought of having a wander in some old building was quite exciting. However, as we got nearer to it, Mum pointed out the circular stone structure rising out of the ground on a large grassy mound and my feelings changed to one of dread, which got worse the nearer I got to it. The tower was built of pale stone so characteristic of York and many people were climbing up the steps to look inside. Mum, by this stage, was walking ahead of me, whilst I held back, not wishing to venture any nearer. The feeling of dread had turned to panic and nausea. Mum called for me to follow her up the stairs, but I couldn't move any closer. She was halfway up them before she realised I was no longer behind her.

'Come on,' she called to me.

I just stood, shaking my head in reply, unable to move any further. After a few moments she descended, looking puzzled.

'I thought you wanted to see some history?'

All I managed to do was to shake my head.

'What's the matter?' Mum's expression changed to one of mild concern. 'Are you feeling alright?'

'No,' I struggled to reply.

'Let's go sit over there.' She pointed to a bench between the tower and a car park. 'What's wrong? You look a bit pale.'

'I feel a bit sick and dizzy,' I answered hastily and breathlessly. I didn't know how I could possibly begin to tell Mum of the feelings I was experiencing since we first set eyes on that tower. I just knew, that something awful had happened there at some point in time, something frightening and sickening; where many innocent lives had been lost and I was picking up this bad energy. Horrible images of people crammed in together within the tower walls, cries and screams for help falling on deaf ears, then the horror of smoke and fire which people tried to put out but failed. Even sat on this bench away from the tower but with it still in view, was enough to affect me. I had to somehow gather my strength together to get away from it. I didn't want to stay here another minute.

Mum suggested that we make our way back, as she could see that I wasn't well. She helped me up and led me away, thankfully, towards the city and our car.

By the time we reached Granny's house I was feeling much better, although the images and smell of burning still lingered, despite trying to think of more positive things.

Whilst Mum made lunch, she asked if I would like to go and chat to Granny, which I was relieved to do, as it would help me to stop thinking about the morning's events.

As I made my way upstairs to meet her, I wondered what you say to an old grandparent you have never met before. Potentially, it could be quite awkward; my mind was already racing ahead, thinking of possible topics of conversation. I gingerly peered around the bedroom door, where the first detail to hit my senses was the distinct smell of lavender oil, which gently permeated the room. Through the diffused afternoon sunlight seeping through the fully drawn light curtains, I caught my first glimpse of my grandma, who lay reclined upon a high bed, against a bank of cushions and pillows. Her long grey hair, which had partly escaped its fastening, hung down against the cushions, making her look almost as though she were posing for her portrait to be painted. On hearing me enter the room, she adjusted her position slightly, raising herself up on the bed a little.

'I'm not asleep, you know… Come in, let's get a closer look at you.'

I moved to the side of the bed nearest the door, she held out her hand and I instinctively reached out to take it, feeling its warmth spread into mine.

'I've waited a long time for this,' she said, her dark eyes searching my face intensely. 'Sit here,' she continued, patting the space near to her on the bed with her free hand, as she seemed reluctant to let me go.

'Well, you look like your dad's side of the family, but that's no bad thing.' She finally released my hand in order to touch my hair, which I wished I had washed last night. 'But not totally; there's a look of your mum there too.'

Granny continued her silent appraisal of my appearance, then, all of a sudden, as though she had tired of looking at me, she withdrew her concentrated gaze and lay back on the cushions.

'What do you think of York then?'

'Seems very nice,' I answered politely.

'Did your mother show you around the city?'

'We had a bit of a look around.' I told her about the places we had seen and what I thought of them.

'Your mother told me she was going to take you to have a look at the walls and Clifford's Tower, what did you think of them?'

'Well, we didn't have time to see the walls, we will have to do that another time.'

'And the Tower?' she asked, looking at me curiously.

'I didn't like it much,' I found myself saying, to my surprise.

'Oh, and why was that then?' Granny May looked at me carefully.

'I just felt a bit unwell at the time,' I said, choosing my words a bit more carefully.

'Well that's something we have in common, because I don't like that place either... and I think you know why, don't you?' Granny May leaned forward, looking at me intently, not in a menacing way, but as though she was really interested in what I was going to say.

The next thing that happened was totally out of character for me, but I felt the need to confide in her, together with the strong sense that I could trust her implicitly, even though this was our first meeting.

'I'm not sure, but it had a horrible atmosphere and, I think, perhaps, some very bad things happened there.'

Granny May closed her eyes and leaned back on the abundant pillows, as a slight smile crossed her lips.

'Yes, you are quite right, my dear. Some terrible things happened there many years ago. In the dark ages the Jews of the city were persecuted and fled to the tower for protection, only they were all killed. What you felt, my child, was the fear and terror these people felt; the energy lingers, but only a few sensitive people can tune into it.'

She reached for my hand again and held it in hers and said: 'I am glad you came.'

Then suddenly and abruptly her mood changed and she released it, as we heard Mum approaching to announce that tea was ready.

EIGHT

That night Cara slept badly again, her night had been full of dreams which she struggled to recall and which left her feeling confused on waking. She couldn't get over Suzann calling her cat Lily; what were the chances of that happening?

Cara knew that her mother reacted to stress and anxiety in a fairly typical way, she baked. She must have found this helped her by focusing on something else. However, as neither of them had much of an appetite at the moment and there was only so many cakes her grandma would eat, so there was already quite a surplus of cakes, breads and biscuits building up, despite giving a lot away. So Meg suggested Cara take some around to their neighbours.

Cara was pleased to find Clive was at home on his own. Eileen had gone shopping, according to her husband, a tall, slim man with a kindly face, framed by a grey beard, which compensated for the lack of hair on his head. He appeared unsurprised by her visit, no doubt his wife had told him that she might pop around. He invited her into the tidy house and offered her a cup of tea, making very complimentary remarks about Meg's baking as he relieved Cara of the bags of biscuits and cake.

'Now, Eileen has told me that you are interested in history, particularly local history. Is that right?' Clive said, getting straight to the point.

Cara confirmed that.

'Well, I've got a few bits and pieces you might be interest in. I will just go and fetch them, whilst the tea is brewing.'

He returned a few minutes later with a large box file, which he opened up on the kitchen table. It was full of papers, diagrams and photographs. He chose a few random items, which he seemed keen to show Cara, whose heart sank when it became apparent that they were all concerning the industrialisation of the area, a subject Clive was evidently enthusiastic about, as he brought out additional photos to illustrate his findings, before going on to show her various places on a large map of the area. At this point, Cara was beginning to regret her visit and was wondering how she could make her escape, without it looking rude. When all of a sudden, he stopped talking and turned to look at her.

'But… you didn't come round here to see all this, did you? You must forgive my rambling on, my enthusiasm for history gets the better of me sometimes. Now what exactly would you like to know?'

Breathing a sigh of relief, Cara explained that she would like to know about the history of her house and all the people who had lived in it.

'Right, well I haven't got that sort of information, I'm afraid. I could tell you when it was built, who built it and probably where the bricks came from.' He laughed. 'But nothing about the occupants.'

Clive must have noticed the look of disappointment register on Cara's face on hearing this, for he added: 'But, leave it with me and I will see what I can dig up.'

The next moment Cara's heart nearly leapt out of her ribcage, as she heard the familiar ring tone her father used on his phone. It was quite distinctive and always made her smile, though she had never known anyone else with the same ring tone.

'Sorry!' Clive jumped up. 'I had better answer this, it's probably Eileen.'

He picked up his mobile.

'Hello... hello...' Cara heard him say repeatedly. 'Strange,' he said moments later. 'It must have been a wrong number. Now where were we? Well, like I said, Cara, leave it with me. I can't promise anything but, I will see what I can find out.'

Cara muttered her thanks and made her way towards the front door, still feeling a little shaken hearing her father's ring tone, then she remembered.

'I couldn't help noticing that you have such a nice garden and it must take a lot of looking after. Does Eileen have someone to help her with it?'

'If Eileen were here,' Clive laughed, 'she would be the first one to tell you that she cannot take any credit for the garden. Oh, she likes to sit in it and admire it alright, usually with a large gin and tonic. But as for working in it, no! So I do it all, another one of my hobbies.' He winked.

Back in her own room, Cara's head was full of confused thoughts. There were so many odd things happening to her lately, so many coincidences. What did it all mean? She wondered about the woman she had seen in Clive's garden. On a whim, Cara decided to revisit the entry in Suzann's diary about Maud. As she read, she felt the goose bumps rise on her arms as she noted the description Suzann had given of Maud wearing a tweed skirt and a cardigan, which matched what she had seen the lady wearing. *Another strange coincidence*, she thought.

That afternoon, Cara had nothing much to do, so she decided to continue reading and turned to the next diary entry. If nothing else, it would stop her thinking and worrying about her dad.

8th August

After that first day, we kind of slipped into a bit of a routine. In the mornings Mum would do some housework, which I helped with, and cooking, which I didn't help with. Instead I would sit with Granny May and listen as she told me a little about herself and the life she had led. It wasn't all one way though; she seemed just as interested in hearing about my life as I was in hers.

It was good to learn more about my family. Granny, unlike Mum was very open and talked freely when I asked questions. Although my mum and Granny shared similar problems, as my grandfather died when Mum was quite young, leaving Granny to manage on her own, just like us really; that was apparently the only thing they had in common. Mum, according to Granny, was: 'More like your granddad. We don't share the same interests.'

We looked at loads of old photos, lots of Mum when she was young, some of which were quite funny. Even Mum, who popped in with a cup of tea for Granny, joined in looking through them and had to laugh at the sight of herself in some of them.

In the afternoons, whilst Granny slept, Mum and I went out together, which I enjoyed, perhaps because she seemed much more relaxed. We visited various places in York; amongst them the majestic Minster, which Mum told me was built above a Roman building. Unfortunately, we didn't have time to go and see it as the remains are buried deep in the bowels of this huge structure. Virtually opposite the Minster, we saw Guy Fawkes' birthplace, which I thought was kind of a pretty neat townhouse and not the sort of place you might expect someone like him to live in. The Jorvik Museum was a good place to visit, as they attempted to take you back to a time when the Vikings settled in York. Mum told me that she could remember them building it, many years ago, when they discovered the remains of a Viking settlement on the site. One afternoon we even had a cruise down the River Ouse, with Mum as my own personal tour guide.

In fact we have been so busy I haven't had time to write.

On Thursday afternoon, Mum took me for a walk on the walls. I had been looking forward to that since we had had to abandon the idea after that first day encounter with Clifford's Tower. You got a good view of the city from there, although it was a bit narrow in places and you had to get off the wall a few times and cross over a road or two. The wall was punctuated by a number of gates which were called 'Bars' and some were quite grand affairs. A few had rooms in which you could walk through. At one such 'Bar' – I have forgotten which one it was – Mum and I were having a good look around following a small group of Japanese tourists. I was preoccupied looking out at the view across the city from one of the small windows, so I hadn't noticed Mum and the other tourists had moved on. I turned around to find the room was empty and so quiet that you couldn't even hear the gentle hum of the traffic below. All of a sudden a little girl bounced into the room, wearing what looked like fancy dress –

a longish tunic in a rather heavy material for this time of year. In fact, I thought to myself, *She must be hot in all that lot!* but kids wear funny things sometimes. Anyway, she seemed excited, smiling at me, then put her finger to her mouth conspiratorially. She was probably playing hide and seek and didn't want anyone to know where she was. I simply smiled back at her, casually glancing past her, expecting to see a load of similarly dressed children about to burst in, but couldn't see anyone, thankfully. I moved over towards what looked like a minute alcove with a small brass plaque above it, when I heard the little girl giggling. Turning around, I saw that she was now standing quite close to me, which wasn't such a good thing as her face looked as if she was wearing a dark foundation or face paint, giving her a distinctly grubby look.

'Shall I tell you a secret?' she said, looking dreadfully pleased with herself.

'If you want,' I said, not in the least interested.

'I've hidden my father's key,' she whispered.

'Have you!'

'Yes, and it's in a place where no one will ever think to look.'

And with that dramatic piece of information she turned and skipped out of the door she had come in by. Almost immediately, I became aware of the noise of the traffic again, the sound of children chattering and the movement of people outside, as a party of children on an outing poured into the room. Making my way to the door at the far end of the room, I turned to see if I could see the little girl with a secret to tell but none of the children were wearing fancy dress, they were all identical in their Brownies uniform.

Outside I met up with Mum, who was studying a guide map. I decided it was best not to mention the little girl I had just seen.

*

That evening, after dinner, Mum went up to Granny's room to clear her tray and settle her down for the night. I hadn't been aware of the length of time that she had been up there because I had been watching the TV. However, on my way up to the bathroom, I could hear Mum and Granny talking not too quietly. In fact, as I got closer to Granny's room door, which was slightly ajar, I could hear them quite clearly. It was only when I heard my name mentioned – it's instinctive, you naturally stop what you are doing and listen. I didn't intend to eavesdrop. As I hovered on the landing, I could hear Granny say: 'She's nothing like you, Maureen. She's got her father's looks but not his personality—'

'Thankfully.'

'She's more like our side of the family... in fact I see a lot of me in her and, I think you can too, if you would only admit it.'

'I'm sure I don't know what you mean.'

'I think you know exactly what I mean, Maureen.'

'Oh don't start all that again, Mum. You know very well what I think of all that stuff and nonsense.'

'The child needs encouragement, Maureen, and understanding, that's all I'm saying.'

'She's OK as she is.' I could detect a familiar tone of impatience in my mum's voice. 'Just leave it alone, Mum. There's nothing to be gained from delving into all this, she's just a normal kid. I don't want you filling her head with all this mumbo jumbo rubbish – I had enough of that, remember, when I was a kid.'

'Maureen, you're wrong.' Granny's voice sounded quite stern, as though she was determined to put her point across. 'So very wrong. Like it or not your child has the gift...'

At that crucial point in the conversation, I must have moved slightly, as the floor board beneath me creaked and they both stopped talking. Fearing I should be caught eavesdropping, I made a dash for the bathroom but, as I was closing the door, I caught Mum's eye as she came out onto the landing.

Somehow I felt I had to justify why I was there, so I found myself ridiculously stating the obvious:

'Just using the bathroom.'

Now, if that wasn't an admission of guilt, then I don't know what is!

10th August

On Friday morning, the day we left for home, Granny May seemed a bit brighter. When I popped in with her breakfast tray she was already sitting propped up in bed, reading a magazine.

'You look a lot better this morning, Granny.'

'Yes love, I'm feeling much better. It must be having you around the place that's done it,' Granny said, taking my hand in hers. 'I can't believe you are going home already; it doesn't seem two minutes since you got here.'

'I know,' I replied, feeling more than a twinge of sadness at the thought of leaving her. 'Perhaps when you are feeling better you could come down and stay with us. Would you like that?'

'That would be nice,' she said, without meeting my eyes.

'You promise to come and see us then?' I asked, giving her hand a slight squeeze.

'I promise I will come and see you,' Granny said, but this time she looked directly at me, so I knew that she meant it.

*

Later that morning, after saying a sad farewell to a granny I had become very fond of in such a short time and, after the morning rush hour had passed, Mum and I set forth on our long journey south. It was largely uneventful and hugely boring, except for some magazines which Granny had given me, together with a bag of sweets, for which I was grateful. Thankfully, I was one of those people who could manage to read in the car without feeling sick. One of the magazines she had given me was a sort of tourist guide book to York, so I settled myself down to read it, remembering the places Mum had taken me. One particular item caught my attention, though. When I was reading an article about the Roman walls, it described the gates or 'Bars' as they call them, or rather one of them in particular, and a story about an event that was supposed to have occurred hundreds of years ago. At that time the gates had gate keepers and their families lived there, as they had to physically open the gates to let people in and out and so were responsible for the security of the city. The story involved one little girl who decided to take her father's keys to the gate and hide them from him. Unfortunately, the girl couldn't remember where she had hidden them and as a result, her father lost his job as gate keeper, and the family lost their home. I thought back to the little girl I had seen at one of the gate houses, who, I had supposed, was in fancy dress, or was she?

*

That night, Cara again slept badly. As in previous nights, her dreams were disjointed, full of faces she did not recognise, with the exception of one, her father. She saw his face clearly and thought she heard him say: 'I'm alright, Cara.'

She woke, shaking as though from a bad nightmare, and immediately burst into tears.

NINE

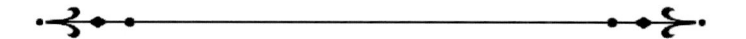

The next day, after lunch, Alicia came round. Her mother dropped her off after Cara, Helen and Meg had made an attempt to eat something. Meg was doing a good job of putting on a brave face in front of her daughter but, Cara wasn't fooled; she could see the tell-tale signs of worry etched across her mother's face, especially when she thought Cara wasn't looking. Likewise, Cara tried to be brave for her mother's sake, only Alicia could see the truth written on her friend's face.

Cara was pleased Alicia was here, especially after what had happened yesterday at Clive's, and was eager to tell her all about it. Alicia too seemed impatient to get upstairs, so after a few polite words had been exchanged with Meg, the two disappeared up to Cara's room.

'I've got some news for you,' Alicia whispered as soon as they were out of earshot of Meg. 'It was a bit of a coincidence, really,' she continued, climbing the stairs.

There's that word again. Cara thought to herself.

'Do you remember Joseph? The chap who helps Mum in the garden.'

Cara struggled to think of anyone of that name.

'You've met him, I know you have. He's about sixty-ish, short, with grey hair and always wears a cap?'

Cara still couldn't place him, despite the helpful description.

'You must remember him.'

'No, I don't. What about him anyway?' Cara said, already fed up with this conversation.

'Well.' Alicia paused whilst she smoothed Cara's unmade bed a little before sitting down on it and continuing. 'He remembers Phil.' Alicia's eyes were wide with excitement. 'Apparently, he used to help out at Durley Manor sometimes during the summer.'

'Who did?'

'Joseph, of course. Keep up, Cara! He worked with Phil and described him just like Suzann had said in her diary too. Isn't that amazing? I suppose this proves she wasn't making it up.'

'All it proves is that there was a gardener at Durley Manor called Phil who lodged with Suzann.'

'But why go to all that trouble of writing a diary based on people she knew and came into contact with but making up the rest? It doesn't make sense. I thought a story is usually fictitious and diaries were almost always about actual events. I only ever put facts in my diary.'

'I know, it's all a bit weird, I just don't know what to make of it,' Cara replied thoughtfully. 'How did you find out anyway?'

'He was over yesterday helping Dad dig out some old hedges and he cut his hand. I was in the kitchen when he came in with Dad, who then went to look for some plasters and then we got chatting. I said that it must be an occupational hazard getting hurt in the garden and he said that it didn't happen that often now. But went on to say, when he first started gardening at Durley Manor, it happened quite a lot, a bit of a clumsy teenager apparently. Anyway, I asked him if he knew Phil. He thought for a few minutes and said yes! He described him as being tall and skinny and a good gardener, just like Suzann had said.

Then Dad came back so I couldn't ask him anything else.'

'Well at least we know he is a real person and not made up. Did you get a chance to ask him any more?'

'No. His cut was quite deep and wouldn't stop bleeding, so Dad had to take him to A and E, which was a shame.'

'Shame about going to hospital or shame about not being able to ask him any more?'

They both laughed.

Cara told her friend about Clive's promise to try and find out about who had lived in their house, but she decided not to mention the strange woman she had seen in her neighbour's garden and her resemblance to Suzann's description of Maud. Neither did she tell her about the vivid dream she had of her father, or Clive's ringtone being the same as her dad's.

The rain which had started not long after Alicia arrived, looked set to continue for the rest of the day, so Alicia suggested they read a bit more of Suzann's diary. So the two friends got themselves comfy on Cara's bed and read the next few entries together.

11th August

I had hoped for a bit of a lie in, as it felt good to be back in my own bed. I could have slept in if it hadn't been for a persistent banging noise which came from downstairs. Poking my head from underneath the covers, I glanced at the alarm clock, which said quarter to nine. I decided it was pointless trying to go back to sleep with all that racket going on, so I slipped on my dressing gown and hunted for my slippers, as they were a necessity when Phil was doing a 'spot of DIY', as he wasn't the tidiest of workers.

I found Phil in the kitchen, with his back towards me, crouched down by the kitchen door. I wondered what on earth he was doing, bits of wood and various tools lay strewn across the floor.

'Morning, Phil,' I said as he obviously hadn't heard me come into the room.

'Oh, hello Suz,' he answered, looking up briefly. 'You had a good time at your granny's?'

'Yes thanks,' I replied. 'What are you doing?'

'I meant to do this whilst you were away in York, but I didn't...' He trailed off as he obviously couldn't think of a suitable excuse. 'Actually it was meant to be a surprise.'

'That's nice, but what is it?'

'I'm making a cat flap for your little kitten.'

He stood up to reveal a small square opening which he had cut out of the back door. Even to my inexperienced eyes, I could see that it wasn't in the right place.

'Isn't it a bit too high?'

'Ah, that's where my little step comes in!' he said, reaching for a small piece of wood which he placed beneath the section he had cut for the cat flap to be inserted. 'She will be able to jump onto this first, and then out through her cat flap – brilliant idea, isn't it?'

I wasn't so sure; how would she get in from the outside and what would Mum say?

Later, whilst munching on some toast and watching Phil make a half-hearted attempt at clearing up his mess, he said: 'Almost forgot, there's a note for you from Hugo, it's in the hall.'

Jumping up, I found it on the hall table. It said:

Dear Suzann,

I hope you had a good time at your grandma's. Phil

told me that you are able to take one of the kittens, which are now ready to be collected. Perhaps, if you are not too busy, we could go riding?

Hope to see you soon.

Best wishes, Hugo

The note was typical of Hugo, quite formal, but it was nice to hear from him and I could pick up my kitten, which was even better. Going back into the kitchen, I asked Phil if he was going over to the Manor. He said he was, so I ran upstairs to change.

*

Twenty minutes later we were rattling down the twisting country lanes on our way to the Manor. On the back seat I had placed a cardboard box with and an old but fluffy towel inside, for Lily. As we were approaching the old gate house, large rain drops appeared on Phil's dirty windscreen, which turned into muddy slurry when he switched on the wipers, so we couldn't see where we were going for a few moments. By the time we had parked the car around by the stable block, the rain was quite torrential.

Dashing into the stables to avoid getting soaked, I saw Hugo, who was tightening the girth on his horse's saddle. He looked up as I approached him.

'Hello, I thought you might come today.'

'It's chucking it down out there, Hugo,' I said, wiping rain drops from my face and patting my hair in the vain hope that it wouldn't frizz.

'Oh well, we can wait here for a few minutes until it stops.'

So we sat on a couple of bales of straw and chatted. He asked me about my trip to York and I was surprised at how easy I found him to talk to; he seemed genuinely interested too. While outside the rain continued to pour down.

After a while, he suggested that we go into the house.

'Could I see my kitten first?'

'Yes, of course.' He led the way into the disused stable Lily's mother had chosen as the 'nursery' for her little ones. It wasn't difficult to spot her as she was the only kitten there. The others, I presumed, had gone to their new homes. She was playing with some straw, stalking and getting ready to pounce at any minute. I noticed how much she had grown in just a week; she also seemed much more independent, hardly seemed to notice when her mother padded off when we entered the stable. I couldn't resist picking her up and giving her a cuddle, feeling the softness of her fur against my face and hearing her purring as I did so. I felt the bond between us growing.

After a few minutes I reluctantly put her down.

'See you later,' I said to her. 'She will be there when I'm ready to go home, won't she?' I asked, worried that she might run off.

'Of course she will. Come on, we will see what Mrs B's been up to in the kitchen. There was a nice chocolaty smell earlier.'

*

In the kitchen, Mrs B was busy clearing out some cupboards when we burst into the room.

'Oh! Take your shoes off, you two – I've just cleaned the floor.'

When we had both done as we had been told, she made us a mug of tea and produced some chocolate brownies from a cake tin, which were still a bit warm. Presumably these were what Hugo had smelt cooking earlier. Mrs B then left us in search of Hugo's father, armed with a mug of tea.

'So when is the shooting weekend?'

'This Saturday. Father has been working hard to ensure everything is in order. There are a number of Americans coming and a few of his friends and contacts are joining in as well. Mrs B has said that she doesn't mind cooking the breakfasts and lunches but she will be having some help with that. So everything is more or less sorted. Father is already thinking about organising another one. If this one goes well we could get a name for ourselves.'

We finished off our tea, then Hugo left me for a few minutes to see his father. Whilst he was gone, I looked out of the large kitchen windows that overlooked the back of the house, hoping that the rain had eased off. I saw it was still raining quite hard, and, what's more there didn't seem to be a break in the clouds either. I was then aware of voices in the hall. Thinking that one of them was possibly Hugo's, I moved nearer to the kitchen door, where I saw a group of men talking to Hugo's father. I recognised a few of them from our village. One was the doctor, another was the vicar and the other was Major Smyth. The reason I recognised them was due to the fact that Mum cleans for them all. They appeared to be talking about the forthcoming shoot in very friendly terms, but no sign of Hugo.

After a while the men disappeared and the hall was once again silent except for the patter of paws as Hector and Paris scampered after Hugo's father, followed by a honey-coloured spaniel. It was looking increasingly likely that there would be no riding today and I was beginning to get restless waiting for Hugo, although I thought it would appear rude of me to go in search of him.

Just when I was beginning to get a bit cross, Hugo burst in, full of apologies.

'Sorry, Suzann. Father wanted me to help sort something for him quite urgently. And it looks like we won't be able to ride today. You are more than welcome to stay. Mrs B is around somewhere, but I'm afraid I have to help Father with some urgent business.'

'That's OK. I kind of thought you had got caught up with something. By the way, I didn't realise you have three dogs, what's the spaniel called?'

Hugo turned and looked at me oddly.

'What spaniel?'

I could have died! So I said, 'I will go and collect my kitten and wait for Phil.' I got up to go, anxious to avoid any questions from him, that I wouldn't be able to answer.

'Father says Phil should be along in about fifteen minutes, as he can't do much in this weather either,' Hugo said as I retreated to the stables.

Actually, although I was a bit disappointed not to be riding today, I couldn't wait to take Lily home, so I went out into the rain to retrieve the box I had made ready from the back of Phil's unlocked car, and then ran into the stable block to find her.

She was all on her own, curled up on the straw next to the now slightly dilapidated cardboard home she had shared with her siblings. It looked as if it had been chewed and crawled over so many times, the sides had flopped over and the whole thing was leaning precariously to one side. All the same I felt quite sad for her to be leaving this place and guilty about taking her away from her mother. In fact, I was worrying about whether I ought to wait until the mother returned before I took her, when I heard a rustling noise coming from the stall next door. Thinking this was likely to be Lily's mother, I got up quietly so as not to startle her, and was just about to peer in, when I saw a man standing a few metres away from me. It was a bit gloomy in the stables as the whole place is lit only from the outside door, which is always open, so I didn't immediately recognise him. I was just initially shocked to see him and couldn't help an involuntary but, very audible, intake of breath; I must have surprised him too, as we both stood looking at each other for a few moments. It was his clothes which betrayed his identity. In particular, the jacket with the string tied around the middle which is very distinctive. He spoke first:

'What are you doing in here?'

'I've come to collect my new kitten,' I said defensively.

'Does the Squire know you're 'ere?'

'Yes.'

'Well, mind you don't touch nothing. Stables can be dangerous places, especially for young 'uns.'

I wasn't sure whether he was referring to me or the kitten, but he then turned and I watched him walk slowly out of the stable block and continue at the same pace outside, as though he was unaware of the rain falling like tiny ferocious spears all about him.

Suddenly, I was aware of a feeling of softness being rubbed against my trouser leg. Looking down, I saw that Lily's mother had returned. I bent to stoke her and tried to coax her in to saying goodbye to her last kitten, but she didn't seem all that interested.

This task kept me absorbed for some time, so I was unaware of Phil coming into the stable.

'Are you ready to go then?' he asked, watching me play with Lily and her mother.

'Yes, whenever you are.'

A few minutes later we were on our way home with Lily secure in her temporary new abode, which I held tightly on my lap in the front seat, as Phil negotiated the potholes with more care than he had done on previous occasions.

When we finally reached home I spent the rest of the day settling her in. She surprised me by doing this with relative ease. The litter tray was also no problem, which pleased Mum. I had bought her a couple of toys whilst out on one of our shopping trips to York market, so the evening was spent playing with her. Mum had insisted that Lily sleep in the kitchen from the start. I had tried to argue against this because she was young and it was her first night here. But Mum was un-moved; in the kitchen she had to remain.

12th August

After yesterday's downpour, I woke up to see sunshine and a blue sky punctuated only by a few stray white clouds. I had offered to help Phil in the garden this morning but hadn't done much when I heard Mum calling me from the house. Dumping the watering can down, I made my way towards the open door.

'Ah there you are,' Mum said, giving me a half smile, which unfortunately didn't bode well. It usually meant that there was a job she wanted me to do.

'How do you fancy earning a bit of money?'

'Yeah, maybe,' I answered cagily.

'Good.' Mum decided to deliberately ignore my hesitance. 'I've been asked to do some cleaning up at the Manor; it seems that they are having a large group of people staying there for the weekend and could do with some help cleaning the rooms. I've said you would help too, seeing as you know them up there. Anyway, it will mean an early start.'

She then returned to the kitchen, which was just as well as I couldn't believe she had volunteered me for the job. How embarrassing is that? What would Hugo think? I would never be asked to go riding there again. I went upstairs before I said something I might regret and to try and think of a way out of this but, short of a mysterious overnight illness, I was at a loss to think of anything.

*

The next morning, we were up early, as Mum had promised and, after a swift breakfast, we were on our way to the Manor in Phil's old Citroen. At first Mum had refused to go in it as it was such a mess, but Phil managed to persuade her by fetching a clean old blanket from the house for her to sit on. I, on the other hand, had to make do with yesterday's newspapers, after I had cleared a space to sit down in between a number of dirty plant pots and a box of gardening tools. However, I was past caring. I was certain Hugo would feel as embarrassed as I was now feeling; also, I had kind of got used to the holiday lie-ins, so it felt like the middle of the night, when in reality it was only ten to seven. I sat back, carefully avoiding the hedge trimmers, listening to Mum's complaints about the state of Phil's car.

'Well I just hope that no one recognises me in this,' she moaned.

I thought it highly unlikely that anyone would, given the time of day.

*

Mrs B met us at the grand arched front door, dressed in her usual brightly coloured apron, and showed us into the impressive hall, where I had been given a detailed tour only a few weeks before.

We waited a few minutes as Mrs B dished out various cleaning implements and issued instructions for use. Then a couple of ladies from the village, who Mum recognised as Janet and Mary, arrived. Mrs B then dispatched us to our various rooms, up the grand staircase and onto the large galleried landing.

According to Mum, making the bed with someone else is much easier and quicker than on your own. I think she must be right, as I hadn't appreciated just how physically demanding it could be. The mattresses were old and some looked to be stuffed with feathers and weighed a ton. We polished antique surfaces carefully, vacuumed and polished bare, ancient-looking floor boards and dusted just about everything in sight. One of the rooms on our list was 'Lady Carlotta's' bedroom and Mum immediately got to work stripping off the old counterpane whilst I hung around by the doorway looking for any sign of the young girl I had seen on my previous visit.

'Come on, Suzann. We haven't got all day, love!'

'Sorry, I'm just not used to it.'

'Never mind, we'll pop down for a tea break after this room. Mrs Burgess said there was tea in the kitchen after 10. Just help me with this, will you?'

Mum was struggling to turn a mattress which was heavy. We wrestled with it for a few minutes before finally getting it into the right position. Then Mum announced that she had to go and find some more sheets, so I sat down on the edge of the bed to recover. Whilst I was getting my breath back, I could have sworn that I heard someone calling my name. Thinking it was Mum wanting some help, I made for the bedroom door but, looking down the corridor, I could see no one. Thinking that I had been mistaken, I turned back into the room; it was then that I heard it again, only this time more distinctly. Looking around the room, I couldn't place where the voice was coming from. Walking to the window, which we had opened to let some fresh air into the room before starting work, I looked to see if it was anyone outside, but there was no one there. Looking back at the room again, I caught sight of the old mirror. I walked up to it and saw my own reflection peering back from the badly worn surface; otherwise the room was empty.

'Hello Suzann.' A soft female voice came from inside the room. I swung around expecting to see the girl sat on the window seat, but there was no one there.

'Suzann!' The voice was faint but unmistakable.

'Who is it?' I asked, searching the reflection in the mirror in the hope of seeing her again.

'It's me, you twerp, who else were you expecting?' Mum's distinctive voice announced her return. She marched into the room with an armful of neatly folded white sheets and pillowcases.

'Is this place giving you the creeps then?'

Yes, er, no,' I stuttered, hardly knowing how to account for the fact that Mum had caught me talking to myself – not for the first time either.

'I think we need a tea break,' she said, placing her bundle down on the bed. 'Come on, Mrs Burgess has the kettle on and with any luck we might get a biscuit.'

As we left, I took one more look at the room. It was empty, but I know what I had heard, I just wondered what she wanted from me.

*

Mum was right, Mrs B had put out some biscuits and some home-made flapjacks. There was a lovely smell of something cooking. The whole room was a hive of activity as Mrs B was busy preparing what looked like biscuits. I seemed to have worked up quite an appetite making beds and was on my second flapjack when Hugo casually walked in, silently helped himself to a biscuit and, after taking a bite, came and sat on the empty chair next to me. I could feel my face turning a bright shade of pink. Thank goodness, Mum was busily chatting to the other ladies about the recent spate of burglaries in the village. I just felt so embarrassed that I was here with my mum cleaning – what must he think? I couldn't even think of anything to say. In the end, he spoke first:

'Glad you decided to come along.'

I wasn't sure whether this was a question, or whether he was glad I was here.

'Mum asked me if I would like to help.'

'Mrs B thought you might like to; it was her idea to ask you.' Somehow that made me feel a bit better. 'She is a bit funny about asking people she doesn't know to the house. I meant to ask you if you would mind giving us a hand the other day, but as you know I got called away and didn't get an opportunity. How are you getting on anyway?'

After giving a brief account of our progress, I asked how the preparations for the weekend were going.

'Fine, thank you. I've been helping Father in the office as he's been quite busy... but we are pretty much on top of things, which is just as well as the guests arrive after lunch. How long are you here for?'

'I'm not sure whether I'm needed tomorrow as well; I will have to ask my mum.' I nodded in the direction of Mum, who was still chatting, as Hugo hadn't met her before.

'Actually, I meant today – what time do you think you will finish?'

'Oh!' I felt myself blushing, feeling stupid. 'I think we will be finished by lunch time; why?'

'Do you fancy going for a ride this afternoon?'

'Could do, I suppose.'

Hugo seemed to take my response as a yes and, after taking another biscuit, jumped up.

'See you later then.'

*

Mum and I continued our work upstairs and finished in good time, which was just as well as I noticed, on our way downstairs, that a few large four-wheel drive cars had pulled up at the front of the house, together with a number of dogs which scampered about. Mum and I made our way to the kitchen to deposit our cleaning tools and, after she exchanged a few words with Mrs B, said cheerio to me. She left, having arranged a lift home with one of the other two ladies. I just hung around the kitchen waiting for Hugo. Mrs B popped in looking a bit hot and flustered. Not long after, Hugo came in and announced that he was 'starving'.

'I'm afraid you will have to fend for yourselves today, I haven't got time,' she said as she disappeared in the direction of the dining room.

'Do you fancy a sandwich?' Hugo said with his head in the fridge.

I sat and watched as Hugo made a large mound of sandwiches. Outside in the hall we could hear the voices of the shooting party chattering loudly and animatedly.

After a speedy lunch, we headed for the stables. Thankfully, I had worn my jeans today and Hugo had a spare pair of gloves, although they were a bit on the large side, so we were all set.

We took a different route so that we were well clear of the shoot, although I was sure we would still be able to hear them, which bothered me. I couldn't bear to think of those beautiful little birds being shot. I know that, morally, I couldn't justify it as I wasn't a vegetarian but it was enough to make me seriously contemplate it.

We galloped across The Chase and ended up by the banks of the River Bourne as it gently meandered through a wide valley. We stopped to let our horses drink from it.

'Can you hear anything?' Hugo asked suddenly.

'No,' I answered, rather puzzled. It was all rather peaceful, just the lyrical sound of the Skylark overhead, climbing ever higher in the clear blue sky.

'Neither can I... Something is wrong – we had better get back.'

'What do you mean?'

Hugo had already started to move away from the stream.

'We should be able to hear the guns from here and I haven't heard a sound.'

'Perhaps the wind is blowing in the wrong

direction?' As I said this, I realised that this was a stupid thing to say, as there was no wind today at all.

We made our way quickly towards the house, the tops of which we could see above the trees, when Hugo stopped abruptly and listened to the silence.

'Perhaps they are having a late start,' I suggested.

'It's nearly half past three!'

I hadn't realised we had been out that long. Maybe his watch was wrong.

As we rounded the corner of the drive and entered the stable yard, I could sense that something wasn't quite right. Hugo quickly dismounted and tied his horse to the railing. I decided to do the same and followed him into the house.

A number of men were gathered in the hall, bags at their feet. Looking at them, you could tell that they were not happy. In the middle of this group was Hugo's father.

'Well Ralph, this is a pretty bad show I must say,' one of the men said.

'Obviously we will want a full refund,' said another.

'Not what you would expect.'

The party began to move towards the door, taking

their bags with them, and started packing up their cars. One or two had already gone, I noticed. Hugo made his way to his father's side and I hung back, feeling a bit awkward. We watched as all the cars disappeared down the drive. Then Hugo and his father retreated into the house deep in thought, leaving me standing alone. Thinking it was time to go, I decided to try and find Phil, which wasn't too difficult, as he was putting some tools away in one of the out-buildings near to the stable.

'What has happened?' I asked him.

'Been a bit of a disaster, if you ask me.'

'I can see that but what happened?'

'No shots – that's what.'

'What do you mean?'

'No bullets for the guns, Suz. Can't have a shooting party without shots, can you?'

'I can't imagine Hugo's father forgetting to order bullets.'

'Shots! No, neither can I. He says he ordered them and that he had them locked away like you are supposed to, but when he went to get them out they were gone.'

'What do you mean?'

'Well that someone must have taken them, I suppose.'

'But I thought you said that they were all locked away?'

'They were, that's the strange thing, because the key wasn't missing and the cupboard the shots were in was locked up alright, just empty.'

'Couldn't he get any more from somewhere?'

'He tried but no one could supply the amount he needed at such short notice. Bit of a shame, as he had spent quite a lot setting this up, cost him quite a bit in other respects too, I shouldn't wonder.'

We got into his car and travelled home together in silence. I couldn't help but wonder how this mix-up had occurred, bearing in mind how much organisation an event such as this would involve: Ensuring that the birds were correctly looked after, then arrangements for the weekend, food and staff. I couldn't imagine that Hugo's father, having gone to such trouble to host an event like this, would overlook one of the crucial elements to its success. But, if that was the case, it meant that someone may have deliberately taken them or hidden them. Somehow this was even harder to believe.

Anyway, one good thing had come out of this if nothing else – the birds hadn't been shot.

15th August

'There's been another robbery in the village, apparently,' Phil said, through a mouthful of toast, scattering crumbs over everything within the near vicinity.

'Where, this time?' Mum enquired from behind the morning paper.

'Up at the Doc's place.'

'Oh no! ...I bet there is a right mess for me to clear up then. It was looking lovely when I left it on Friday. You'd think the police would have caught the culprits by now. That must be the fourth or fifth burglary in the last couple of months.'

'Did they take much?' I asked casually.

'I'm not sure; I heard it from Rob when I was down at the newsagents earlier.'

At that moment, the phone in the hall rang. Mum rushed to answer it.

'What are you up to today, Phil? Are you going to the Manor?' I asked hopefully.

'Sorry Suz, not today. It's my day at the Major's place and then on to Mrs Granger's, as she's asked me to dig up some old roses – I hope she isn't going to throw them away.'

I couldn't help feeling disappointed as I had nothing planned today and would be bored on my own. Besides which, I wanted to hear how things were at the Manor after the disaster at the weekend. Mum then returned with the news that she had been asked to go over to the doctor's house to help clean up after the burglary. Worse was to follow as she asked me to go along and 'help'. The day looked like it was going downhill rapidly.

*

Mum had worked for Doctor and Mrs Fitzgerald for about four years, ever since they had moved into the area and taken over the practice.

The doctor's house occupied a prime position in our village. There were a few houses that were set back from the road, with tall hedges either side of twin wrought iron gates. The houses were partly obscured from view but, according to Mum, the doctor's house was probably the grandest. As we walked down the immaculate drive towards the shiny black front door, with stone columns either side and pretty flowers growing in colour co-coordinated tubs, it reminded me of a large doll's house. I was about to mount the four stone steps to the front door, when Mum grabbed my arm and steered me towards the back of the house and the kitchen door, where the doctor's wife met us. Mrs Fitzgerald was quite tall for a woman, or maybe it was the way she stood or her high-heeled shoes. She was dressed in a pale grey skirt with a pink and grey blouse under a pale pink cardigan, pinned to which was a beautiful brooch with a red stone in the centre. It looked very expensive.

'Ah! Good morning, Maureen – how are you today?' she managed to enquire without giving the faintest indication that she was the least bit interested in how Mum was feeling.

'I see that you have brought along a little helper this morning,' she continued in her distinctly posh accent.

'Good morning, Mrs Fitzgerald. Sorry to hear about the break-in. Where would you like me to start?'

'The study – if you would be so kind, I'm afraid

they made a bit of a mess. The police have done what they needed to do, so it's fine to go in but be careful as there is some glass all over the floor where they broke into the cabinet. Then if you could do upstairs as usual, Maureen, thank you.'

'Did they take much then?' Mum enquired.

'Just some family silver – sentimental value really, and a bit of jewellery. It's all simply dreadful to think someone has invaded our home and gone through our belongings.' Mrs Fitzgerald looked and sounded quite upset, as she turned and dabbed her eyes with a neatly folded lace handkerchief.

'Well, as I said, I'm very sorry for you. Now, perhaps we ought to make a start, if that's alright with you? Now come along, Suzann, I will show you where we keep the cleaning things. Follow me,' Mum said awkwardly.

We collected our cleaning things from a cupboard in the hall and made our way into the study. I was surprised by how little mess there was. I had imagined every drawer and cupboard emptied out onto the floor, but there was none of that here, in fact there was little evidence that a burglary had taken place at all, except for a broken pane of glass from an antique cabinet, which Mum soon vacuumed up. Mum must have been thinking the same.

'They must have known where to look to get the silver. Still, we'll give it a good dust and polish then we are done in here.'

That didn't take us long, thankfully.

On my way upstairs I couldn't help noticing that the house was immaculate. I thought our house was clean, but this one was in a league of its own. Antiques gleamed and gilt-edge mirrors sparkled; soft, inviting-looking cream sofas looked like they had never been sat on. Nothing was out of place; in fact there couldn't be much for Mum to clean, it all looked so perfect.

The main bedroom felt very regal. The centrepiece was a large bed with green-coloured satin curtains behind the bed head, which draped beautifully at either side and were tied back with thick gold cord complete with tassels. It reminded me of pictures I had seen of a throne room. Like the study, there was little sign that a burglary had taken place.

Mum got to work with the vacuum cleaner and, after a few minutes, the carpets resembled a mown lawn. I dusted but there wasn't much furniture in the room, so it didn't take me long. Above the large chest of drawers a picture caught my eye; it was an old sepia photograph of a man and woman in old-fashioned dress. The woman was seated on a chair, the man stood behind; neither of them were smiling.

'How are you getting on?' Mrs Fitzgerald appeared in the doorway.

'We are just about done.'

'Excellent,' Mrs Fitzgerald said, smiling in my direction. 'Well, if you would excuse me, I need to change,' she continued, walking towards the chest of drawers. That was obviously our cue to leave!

I waited on the landing whilst Mum quickly cleaned the bathroom, then we were finished, thank goodness. Even though the house was beautiful and tastefully decorated and probably worth a small fortune, especially when you take into account all the antiques and pictures, it didn't feel like someone's home. It wasn't for me, that's for sure; it would have been like living in a museum and I for one couldn't wait to get out.

TEN

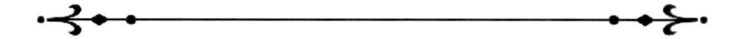

Later, when Alicia had gone home, Cara reflected on the fact that she had never had so many secrets she had not shared with either her mother or her best friend, and she wasn't sure why.

Maybe it was that there were so many odd things happening to her, that on the face of it, were merely nothing but coincidences. Like the music in the car and her father's initials on the registration plate, they could easily be dismissed. Yet, Cara thought about other things that couldn't so easily be explained away, the main one being finding the diaries themselves. Why, after all this time, had they not been found before? Why her? There were similarities between Cara and Suzann, they were both an only child, about the same age too. Suzann's father is absent from her life, or so it seems, and Cara's. Here she stopped trying to analyse things as she tried to block out the worry of her father from her mind. Instead, she decided to look up the meaning of the word 'coincidence' and found it an accurate description of the weird events that had been happening to her but, it failed to explain why:

'…act of coinciding; the occurrence of an event at the same time as another event, without any apparent connection.'

Feeling even more confused, Cara once more felt drawn to continue reading the diary, hoping it would provide her with some answers.

18th August

I have been 'house bound' for the last couple of days as it has rained almost continuously and, except for a shopping trip with Mum, it's been pretty boring. Although, when we returned from the supermarket there was a note for me evidently from Hugo on the hall table in Phil's handwriting asking if I would like to go for a ride the next day. So the first thing I did this morning was to draw the curtains to check on the weather. Outside the gardens were damp; it looked like it had rained during the night but, thankfully, it was fine.

Throwing on an old pair of jeans and a T-shirt and rushing downstairs, I bumped into Phil in the kitchen as he was preparing his usual salmon paste and pickled onion sandwiches for his packed lunch. I reminded him that he was supposed to be giving me a lift to the Manor today, which was just as well, as I think he had forgotten.

Ten minutes later we were on our way. It looked like the day was going to be fine, the clouds were beginning to clear and the sun was shining down on the damp roads, creating small pockets of steam which rose from the tarmac.

As we rounded the corner of the long precarious driveway and the Manor came into view, Phil spotted the two police cars first:

'Hello! What's going on here then?'

'I hope everything is alright,' I said, quickly getting out of the car and making my way to the stables, hoping to find Hugo. After a few minutes searching it was clear that he wasn't there, so I made my way to the kitchen, which was also empty but I decided to wait there. After a few minutes I heard voices in the hall; one I recognised as Hugo's father, the other voice was saying: 'Well, I think we're just about finished here, Ralph. There's not much more we can do at this stage. I'll be in touch.'

'Thank you, Alan. Good of you to come. Cheerio.'

I heard the front door close and a heavy sigh as Hugo's father passed the kitchen end of the hall. Then I turned around to find Hugo had crept silently into the room and was standing only a few metres away, which startled me.

'Oh! Will you stop trying to frighten me all the time?' I said, sounding more cross than I actually felt.

'I thought you had heard me, or were you listening to something else?'

Feeling acutely embarrassed that he had caught me eavesdropping, I asked why the police were here.

'It was our turn to be burgled.'

'Oh no! ...Did they get away with much?'

'Not really, a few bits of silver and some odds and ends but nothing of any real value, thankfully. They did make a dreadful mess in Father's office though. Probably looking for money, turned out all the drawers and book shelves, but they won't find any here, that's for sure.'

'Can I do anything to help?'

After a moment's hesitation Hugo suggested that I could help him sort out the mess in the gallery, if I didn't mind, which I didn't.

On our way, I asked Hugo what had happened.

'It looks like the thief got in through one of the windows in the butler's pantry, which wouldn't have been difficult as they are old and really need replacing.'

'Didn't the alarm go off?'

'No, because we don't have one. Father has looked into it but it would cost a small fortune to secure a place as big as this. He says that he cannot remember the house ever being broken into.'

'Didn't you hear anything in the night?'

'No, because we sleep at the other end of the house.'

By then we had arrived at the gallery, which as the name suggested, resembled a rather long corridor, with windows along one side looking out towards the side of the house. On the opposite wall, there were a number of paintings of various sizes and, to my inexperienced eyes, different styles too. A few were portraits of people who looked like they had been dead for centuries, here and there stood the odd sculpture mounted on stone columns. A few antique-looking chairs were dotted about, which kind of gave it the feel of an art gallery. It was here that we found Mrs B, on her hands and knees carefully picking up bits of broken china from the floor.

'Hello, dear,' she said, looking up. 'What a mess they've made.'

I asked if there was anything I could do to help and she said I could help pick up the pieces, which she was carefully saving just in case the vase could be repaired as it was quite old. Like three hundred years old! It was later whilst I was dusting towards the bottom end of the gallery that I noticed one of the pictures was missing.

'There seems to be a picture missing here,' I shouted to Hugo who was rearranging some furniture at the opposite end.

'Oh, my goodness,' gasped Mrs B when she saw the gap on the wall. 'Well, it was definitely here when I cleaned last week. I had better go and get your father.'

After a few minutes she returned with Hugo's father.

'My, my, looks like the thieves took this as well,' he said, looking a bit puzzled. 'Can't think why they took that one, for goodness' sake; they obviously don't have much of a clue about art. The one above it is worth quite a lot of money – lucky for us.'

'Which picture did they take?' Hugo asked.

'Edmund,' Hugo's father answered, already retreating down the gallery. 'I'll be in my office if anyone wants me.'

Looking at Mrs B and Hugo, I could see that the tension had evaporated. Mrs B was about to attack the carpet with the most ancient-looking vacuum cleaner in existence – the sound was quite deafening. I wondered who this Edmund was but it would be impossible to ask Hugo anything above the noise of the machine. Hugo was already making his way out of the long gallery so I decided to follow him. When we had got far enough away, I asked him who Edmund was.

'He was my father's uncle,' he said, quite matter-of-fact.

'Was? Do you mean he is no longer living?'

'I believe so.'

'Your father didn't seem all that sad that it had been stolen, wasn't he particularly close to him?'

'No.'

'It seems odd that they should steal a picture that isn't worth much. Was it a good portrait?'

'I don't think so.'

'Perhaps they liked the look of it.'

'I don't know why – it wasn't anything special. Just a picture of my grandfather's brother.'

That seemed odd. Why would someone steal a picture that wasn't worth much?

'What did Edmund look like? Was he particularly good looking?' I asked.

'He was supposed to be at the time.'

'I would like to see a picture of him; do you have another painting of him?'

'No, we don't, this was the only one we had.'

We walked in silence together for a little while through a part of the house I hadn't seen before. It looked totally unused, as white dust sheets shrouded pieces of furniture so that they resembled eerie ghostly figures; I was glad it was daylight. In order to break the silence, I asked: 'Did you know your grandfather's brother?'

'No, he died a number of years ago.'

'He must have lived in this house then, along with your grandfather?'

'Yes.'

'Did your grandfather have any other brothers or sisters?

'No.'

Blimey, this was hard work! Hugo must have his mind on the robbery, as he usually doesn't need much prompting to talk at length about his ancestors.

After a short while we emerged into a part of the house I recognised, the first floor galleried landing, when Mrs B called to Hugo to help her move something or other, in one of the rooms further down the corridor.

'I won't be a minute,' he said, rushing off in the direction of Mrs B's voice.

Looking out over the balustrade at the hall below, I surveyed the room with its impressively high beamed ceiling and its chequered black and white tiled floor, wondering at all the people who must have passed through this room since it was first built. Like any old building, it will have been witness to fortunate times as well as tragic and I was beginning to think about Hugo's great-grandparents, when I was aware that someone was standing very close behind me. I could almost feel their breath on the back of my neck. Turning around slowly, I saw the girl I had seen in Lady Carlotta's room standing in front of me. She was wearing a dress of pale pink with little pink rose buds of a slightly darker shade around the neck line, which matched the satin sash around her waist. Because she was so close to me, I could see that we were about the same height, although she looked slightly older than I remembered. She smiled, then spoke:

'Hello, I've been watching you!'

'I know.'

'What do you think of my house?' she said, waving a magisterial arm around.

'It's very nice. What is your name?'

'Carlotta...'

I quickly looked away as I could hear Hugo's footsteps thumping down the corridor towards us. Turning back, Carlotta had disappeared, leaving behind a faint but distinctive smell of lavender.

'Come on, let's get a drink... and seeing as you are

so inquisitive about my relations, I will tell you what I know about Edmund, but it's not something that we talk about too often, so I would appreciate it if you keep it to yourself, OK?'

'Sorry, Hugo,' I said, suddenly feeling embarrassed that I had been so nosey. 'I didn't mean to pry.'

As we made our way across the hall, I glanced back to look at the gallery to see Carlotta smiling down at me. What caught my attention, causing me to stop in my tracks, was through the banisters, I thought I could see a honey-coloured spaniel standing at her side. So that's who it belongs to – well, that's one mystery solved.

A few minutes later, when we were both seated at one end of the large kitchen table, sipping a mug of hot chocolate, Hugo told me about his great uncle Edmund.

'My great-grandfather, Ralph, had twin boys, Maxim and Edmund, but they were not identical. In fact they couldn't have been more different.

'Where Edmund was out going and confident, loved hunting, fishing and other outdoor sports; Max was more studious and reserved. As they grew up, their differences became more obvious, as Edmund regularly got Max into trouble, and generally did what he liked. His mother adored him and I suppose he knew he had her 'wrapped around his little finger', so he got away with most things, although he was also clever enough to push the blame onto someone else.

'Max did very well at school apparently, and went to Oxford University but Edmund wasn't keen on much outside of his own interests and amusements. There were rumours of heavy drinking, trouble with girls and he also started running up large gambling debts.

'Anyway, things came to a head one weekend. Edmund got into trouble with the police and Great-grandfather was left to sort it out. Unfortunately, it was reported in all the newspapers at the time, something to do with gambling, I think. The whole thing nearly ruined us. Great-grandfather had had enough; he read him the riot act and sent him abroad for nine months hoping that he would sort himself out.'

'And did it do the trick?'

'Quite the opposite, really. I suppose, being away from home and having too much freedom. He ran up huge gambling debts, which nearly cost us our home.

'Great-grandfather had to sell off a lot of land, a few farms and other property in order to pay off those debts. As you could imagine it caused no end of stress and worry to my great-grandparents and, because he was in a foreign country at the time, it wasn't easy to sort out.

To make matters worse, after his debts had been settled, Edmund revealed that he had married a penniless girl. So that was the last straw for my great-grandfather. Edmund was sent back to England and promptly disinherited.'

'Was it so bad that he had married a local girl?'

'Well, it was in those days; they were expected to marry well. I suppose, as Edmund had caused so much grief by gambling away so much money, the least he could have done was to marry someone with good family connections.'

'Perhaps he really loved this girl.'

'I doubt it. Apparently, he married her after he got drunk one night.'

'What happened to him after that?'

'No one is quite sure... but the whole episode had a dramatic effect on the family – not to mention our finances. All I know is that my great-grandfather refused to have any more to do with Edmund.'

'That's a bit of a sad story, really.'

'Imagine what would have happened though, if Edmund had inherited this place. He would have lost it within a very short space of time. I don't think my great-grandfather had any other choice.'

'Yes, I suppose so,' I answered thoughtfully.

After a few minutes' silence, Hugo suggested we make our way to the stables. Together we saddled the horses, then led them into the courtyard where we mounted and headed off in a southerly direction.

It felt good to be out. My confidence had increased with every ride and, with it, my fear had vanished. Instead, I enjoyed the adrenaline rush as we raced across open fields; I even managed to jump a small hedge and still remain in my seat. The day was sunny and warm with a few white fluffy clouds scattered across an otherwise clear blue sky. We disturbed a group of fallow deer who were sitting camouflaged, against a backdrop of dry long-stemmed grasses and tall willowy shrubs. They then lolloped off to find somewhere else to secrete themselves. I'm not so sure who was the more startled, them or us. Hugo had to steady his horse, who was a bit unnerved at the sight of them. Other than the deer, though, we saw no one whilst we were out.

We rode quite hard, which meant that there was little opportunity to talk, so I thought about the information Hugo had shared with me about his family. I could understand now why the Manor looked a bit neglected. At the same time, I couldn't help but feel sorry for his great-grandparents. Although their actions sounded a bit harsh to me, it was a different time then with different values, so it becomes almost impossible to put yourself in their position. And what of Edmund? His bad fortune became Max's and, ultimately, Hugo's good fortune. Mine too, as otherwise I wouldn't be here enjoying this ride.

20th August

A bit of a boring day today, I had to go and help Mum over at the vicarage. Mrs Raymond, the vicar's wife, was away looking after her sister in Wales, who was recovering from an operation. The vicar had phoned Mum in a bit of a panic:

'Could you pop around and help tidy things up a bit before she gets back?'

I really didn't want to go, but Mum was a bit

nervous about leaving me at home for any length of time because of all the burglaries in the village. As an incentive, Mum promised me a bit of extra pocket money if I came along. How could I refuse?

The weather wasn't good either, which rather matched my mood; a persistent drizzle which blew in all directions, soaking everything in sight. Despite having an umbrella we were wet by the time we arrived at the front door and even wetter by the time the vicar got around to answering it. Mum was about to knock for the third time when the familiar chubby face of the vicar peered around the door.

'Ah, Maureen,' he said, opening the door for us to escape any further drenching. 'Hello Suzann. Oh, my! How you have grown. Let me take your things. What dreadful weather today, not what you expect for August, is it?'

The vicar chattered, barely pausing for breath, it seemed to me, while he put away our jackets and umbrella and led us into the kitchen. I wondered who the cook was in this household, because it was apparent to anyone walking in here that one of them loved cooking. An old blue Aga was positioned along one wall with brightly coloured tea towels hanging from the door rails. Above it, hung from the open beams, was a selection of cooking implements of all shapes and sizes. At the opposite end of the room, an impressive collection of cookery books was neatly arranged in a large bookcase. It gave the impression of being the centre of this house, and had a lovely feel to it.

The vicar then proceeded to give us a full conducted tour of the rest of the vicarage, pointing out interesting features of the house and some of its contents along the way; very much like an estate agent might do when trying to sell to prospective buyers. Except we weren't and I was already bored, fed up, and just wanted to get it over with.

With the exception of the kitchen, the rest of the vicarage was quite dark, with small windows and low beamed ceilings, which made it feel a little claustrophobic. Even though some of the rooms were quite spacious, they were cluttered with large pieces of dark antique furniture.

Eventually, after we had refused his offer of a cup of tea, he collected the cleaning things we would need and explained, for the umpteenth time, what he wanted us to do, but rather than leave us to it, he persisted in loitering in the doorway, chatting to Mum about local issues as we worked. To make things worse, there was some dreadful organ-type music droning on in the background. The noise was audible throughout the house. It was as though the very walls themselves were acting like speakers, amplifying the sound, so that it was impossible to escape it.

I was hardly aware of what they were talking about, until I heard my name mentioned:

'...Well, of course, our Suzann has spent a lot of time up at the Manor, as she's quite a pal of Hugo's, you know.'

Parents certainly know how to embarrass you! I hate it when she talks about me like that and, in her posh 'telephone voice'!

'Oh, so she knows all about the fiasco of the Grouse shoot then,' I heard the vicar reply. 'I'm afraid he upset quite a number of people that day. Things don't seem to be improving much either, from what I've heard. Still, I hope he manages to turn things around, it would be a great shame if the Manor had to be sold.'

'Sold!' I found myself blurting out before I could stop myself.

The vicar, surprised at my sudden outburst, turned his full attention to me and looked at me with his all-seeing, slightly protruding eyes, which looked like they wouldn't miss a thing.

'Well, I would have thought that, perhaps, Hugo may have mentioned it to you on one of your many visits there.' He continued to hold me in his gaze. 'They can't keep a place like that going without money, and a house that size needs a lot of it. They have no option, if you ask me. Best get rid of it, no point in being sentimental; at the end of the day you have to be practical.'

'But it's been in the family for hundreds of years!' I replied, sounding far more emotional than I intended. 'At least Hugo's father is trying to turn things around.'

'Quite so, quite so, but they haven't had much luck with their various ventures, have they? So what does that tell you?' the vicar asked, with one heavy eyebrow raised. He continued his hypnotic stare, almost as though he were trying to read my thoughts.

'Well goodness me, it that the time? Suzann, we had better get on, it's nearly lunch time,' Mum broke in.

'Is it really?' Vicar Raymond said, his face once again breaking into its usual jovial expression, perhaps in anticipation of lunch. 'Well, I will leave you two ladies to it, as I have to get ready for Mrs Squires' baptism. I don't want to be late for that, do I?'

When he was safely out of earshot, Mum sighed:

'God; that man can talk for England. Come on, let's get finished off here.'

Thankfully, we were only there for a further half an hour and the vicar was so engrossed in his baptism preparations, that he didn't detain us when Mum poked her head around the study door to say goodbye.

*

Later, when I was lying on the bed in my room, watching Lily curled up asleep on her blanket, I kept thinking about what the vicar had said about Hugo's father having, perhaps, to sell the Manor. I hadn't realised that things were as bad as that; no wonder they were pinning their hopes on the shooting party.

21st August

Hugo rang and left a message for me yesterday, when we were at the vicarage. He wondered if I would like to go over today. We hadn't anything else planned so – why not?

Phil dropped me off and said he would pick me up later, as he was working at the garden centre today. I found Hugo with Mrs B in the kitchen. There was an air of excitement; Mrs B had the distracted look of someone with a great deal to do. She barely acknowledged me when I said hello. The work tops were cluttered with cooking implements and an assortment of ingredients littered the usually clear kitchen table. That and the smell of food cooking, suggested to me that something was going on.

Hugo was wrestling with a large carton of cereal, which he successfully opened but managed to spill quite a lot of it all over the place. This minor incident triggered a stern telling-off from an overwrought Mrs B. Feeling a bit sorry for him, I went to help clear up.

'What's going on?' I asked, as I scooped up handfuls of 'Coco Beans' from the floor.

'We are hosting a private dinner tonight for eighteen people; a few local dignitaries and some Americans over here on business. Father seized on the opportunity to offer them a real taste of history, so they are eating here tonight.'

'No wonder Mrs B looks harassed.'

'I don't know why; she's only making the canapés.'

'What are they?'

'They are sort of nibbles you have with drinks before the meal.'

'Oh!' I said, feeling a bit stupid. 'So who is doing the cooking?'

'Father has organised caterers; they cook everything in their kitchens and bring it all here ready to serve, more or less, and then take all the dirty things away with them. They even bring in all the crockery, glasses and the waiters. All we supply is the room. It's a good idea, don't you think? It should be quite a little money spinner for us too.'

At that moment Hugo's father wearily poked his head around the door. After saying hello, he asked if he could 'borrow Hugo' for a few minutes.

Mrs B, who was busily engrossed in counting cutlery, gave me the distinct impression that she didn't want to be engaged in too much conversation, and, as the minutes ticked by and Hugo still hadn't reappeared, I asked her if there was anything I could do. So I helped her polish silver salt and pepper pots; then she taught me how to fold the beautiful white linen napkins which had been starched to within an inch of their lives. We polished the cutlery with tea towels then took it through to the dining room where Mrs B showed me how she would like it all set out on the huge crisp white table cloth and, between us, we laid the table. When we had finished it looked like something from a magazine. In the centre of the table, Mrs B had placed a magnificent flower arrangement, some of the shades of which echoed the colour scheme of the room. One of the last jobs to be done was to place beautifully written name cards by each place setting so that each guest knew where they were sitting. In order to do this, Mrs B referred to a sheet of paper, apparently called a 'seating plan', which had a diagram of the table drawn on it, around which guests' names had been written. It was my job to make sure the name cards were placed in the right places. I noticed a couple of 'Right Honourable', on the list but, I didn't recognise many of the names except for Mr Bradley the local architect, the Major, Reverend and Mrs Raymond and the doctor and his wife.

'Well done, my dear,' Mrs B said when I had finished. 'You've been a great help.' She smiled for the first time that morning; she was obviously feeling a bit less stressed. 'Right, I had better go and pin this on the board in the hall, then everyone can check it when they arrive. Why don't you pop and see if you can find Hugo?'

Following Mrs B into the hall, I stopped to listen for any sound that might indicate where he might be, but except for the noise of Mrs B's shoes on the cold marble tiles, it was silent.

'He may be upstairs, Suzann. I thought I heard him go up there not long ago.'

At first, I felt a bit awkward walking around someone else's house on my own, but this was no ordinary house. Gradually, I relaxed a bit and started to enjoy the freedom to go more or less where I pleased.

I wandered around looking into rooms which I didn't remember seeing, admiring the views from their windows and, before long, I found myself in a part of the house which I didn't recognise. There was no carpet on the corridor floor; no pictures lined the walls; the rooms were either completely devoid of furniture or else it was covered with large dust sheets. Obviously this was part of the house which they hadn't used for a long, long time.

While I was looking out of a window, trying to work out which part of the house I was in, I thought I heard a noise. It seemed to be coming from further down the corridor. Stopping to listen, I heard a faint, intermittent, muffled sound. It was difficult to determine exactly what it was but, the nearer I got, it was clear to me that it was the sound of a human voice. It sounded like someone crying. At the end of the stark corridor, a staircase wound to another floor from where the noise seemed to be coming from.

Slowly, I mounted the staircase. At the top there was a small landing with two doors leading off; one of these was slightly ajar, so it was this one that I peered cautiously into first.

The room was large and well lit from three windows running along the left side. They had distinctive arches at the top and there were two horizontal metal bars running across the glass; this must have been an old nursery. At the far end, two wing-backed chairs partially obscured a fireplace in the centre of the wall. The right-hand chair was covered by a ghostly white dust sheet, but the other was occupied by a man. From my position by the door, I could see him quite clearly; his head was bent, giving him a distinctly round-shouldered look. That gave me the impression that he was an old man. His attention was fixed on something he was holding in his hands, but I couldn't see what it was. He seemed unaware of my presence in the room, so I moved a bit closer. As I did, a wave of sadness came over me and I could see the pained expression etched across his lined face as he studied what looked like an old photograph in his hands. Although I couldn't see it in enough detail, it looked like a family photograph; there were four figures, a man, a woman and two young children – boys, I think, but I couldn't be sure.

In the distance, I could hear my name being called, so faintly at first that it was hardly audible. It was difficult to work out where the voice was coming from; it wasn't anywhere in the room. The voice was getting louder and seemed to be coming from over by the window. Temporarily forgetting about the old man, I went over to the windows and looked out onto the back garden. There below I recognised Hugo, who was walking along across the lawn and calling out my name. Suddenly, I felt like a trespasser and stepped back from the window in case Hugo saw me. It would be difficult to explain to him what on earth I was doing in this part of the house. Turning to leave this sad old man with his memories, I made my way towards the door and crept quietly down the stairs, praying that I would remember how to get back to the main part of the house, before I bumped into Hugo.

Fortunately for me, it was relatively easy to find my way back to the main part of the house, and I almost ran along the bare corridors. A few minutes later, I slowed to a walk along the main upstairs gallery, where Hugo found me.

'There you are, I've been looking all over for you!'

'And I have been looking for you, too,' I replied, trying to sound casual.

'Oh well, you're here now,' Hugo continued. 'It's lunch time, shall we grab something to eat before we go out? I'm starving.'

I agreed that this was a good idea, and we made our way towards the kitchen.

'So where did you get to?' he asked, whilst scrutinising my face almost suspiciously.

'I might ask you the same question. You were gone ages.' The best form of defence is attack, so they say!

'Yeah, sorry about that. Father wanted me to help putting some information together about the house and its history for the guests tonight.'

After a quick lunch, as Mrs B was preoccupied with preparations for the evening, we set out for our ride.

This was, unfortunately, shorter than I would have liked because of the late start, my prearranged pick-up time with Phil and the fact that Hugo needed to be back in good time to help his father.

On my way home, my thoughts drifted back to my exploration of the unused part of the house, especially the old man clutching his photograph. Remembering his intense feelings of sadness and also of loss, I wondered who he was.

ELEVEN

The next morning Cara woke and noticed that it was nearly 9am, which was late for her, not that it mattered as it was the holiday. Despite reading for quite a while last night, she felt surprisingly alert and refreshed after a night free from disjointed dreams. Her grandma had promised to take her out shopping later, so she quickly got herself up. She had just reached the first-floor landing when she became aware of voices downstairs which she did not recognise. Peering over the bannister, Cara caught her breath when she saw a man and woman both dressed in army uniforms standing in the hall talking to her mum. She stopped breathing whilst she strained to hear what was being said, whilst at the same time dreading what she might hear, which as it happened wasn't very much.

'...We will send a car around to pick you up and will be in touch, Mrs Wade, regarding the exact time. Goodbye.'

After Meg had closed the door after the visitors had left. Cara saw her mother cover her face with her hands, her shoulders shuddering in that tell-tale fashion. Cara anxiously flew down the stairs towards her mum, who looked up towards her through her tears.

'He's alright, Cara,' she sobbed, clutching her daughter tightly. 'He's coming home.'

*

The rest of the day passed in a whirl of excitement and anticipation. Meg was almost permanently attached to her mobile as they all waited for more news. Grandma had explained as simply as she could that her father had been involved in a secret mission that went badly wrong, some people had been injured, some killed, and it had been thought that her father had been one of them but, he had managed to escape and was forced to go into hiding. She was over the moon when told that he was being flown home the next day after a thorough health check.

*

It was around lunch time that Cara's phone buzzed signalling a text message; her heart leapt when she saw who it was from.

Hi pumpkin,

Flying back later today, be with you tomorrow, can't wait.

Love Dad xxx

The rest of the day was spent helping her gran and mum get the house looking its best, as it would be the first time her father would have seen it since they had moved in, and later they went into Fordingham, to buy his favourite foods and a few little presents for him.

On their return, there was a large brown envelope addressed to Cara, lying on the door mat. Cara quickly opened it, wondering at first who it could be from but, soon realised when she saw a list of names and dates that it was from Clive. The brief note attached confirmed this, stating that he had managed to get a list of all the previous owners of their house, adding however, that it would not include any people who may have been tenants. She instinctively looked at the names which related to the late 1960s to the 1970s and saw that the house was owned by a Mr J. Bartlett from 1964 to 1980, which didn't tell her much. Disappointed, she replaced the sheet back in the envelope, wondering if that could be Suzann's father's name. Not sure what she could do next, she decided to ask Clive when she went round to thank him.

It wasn't until later in the evening that Cara had some time alone and picked up the diary again. Although all the worries and concerns she had faced yesterday had now evaporated, she was still curious to see how things were progressing in Suzann's world.

24th August

Yesterday, I bumped into Hugo in Fordingham, our nearest small town. Mum left me to mooch around the few interesting shops there, whilst she was in the hairdressers, which normally wouldn't take long. The town centre consists of one main street – The High Street – and that's about all. I did have a particular reason to be in the town, as it is Mum's birthday in a couple of weeks and I hadn't a clue what to get her. I was peering into a ladies' clothes shop window for inspiration, although I don't know why, as most of the things I saw were way beyond my purse – and probably Mum's as well judging by the price tags.

'It's not your colour!' a voice from behind me

startled me. Swinging round, I saw Hugo was standing grinning at me. He was clutching a few bags which suggested he was also shopping. After a few minutes of polite chit-chat, he offered to buy me a drink at 'The Cosy Café'.

Typically for a Saturday morning, the café was busy. Luckily, just as we walked in a couple were leaving a nice window seat overlooking the High Street. Hugo ordered a milkshake and a doughnut and I had the same. After a few moments' silence, as we both savoured our sugary doughnut, trying hard not to squirt jam everywhere, Hugo seemed a bit distracted. He kept his eyes focused on the remains of his doughnut, absentmindedly creating swirls in the sugary crumbs on his plate.

We sat in silence for a few moments. I sensed that there was something he wanted to tell me, as it was clear he had things on his mind.

'How did the dinner party go?'

'Not very well. Father thought everything was going too smoothly. The dining room was looking terrific; we were all organised. The guests all arrived on time, dressed in their "best bib and tucker" and Mrs B did a marvellous job with the canapés.'

'So what happened?'

'We had no food.'

'What do you mean? I thought you had caterers?'

'Well, that's what we thought. Father had it all booked; they sent us some menus and we discussed it with them. When they didn't turn up, Father rang them and they told us that someone had rung a few days earlier and cancelled our booking, which is rubbish, because we hadn't.'

'So if it wasn't you who cancelled, who was it?'

'We don't know. That's the worrying part, why would anyone do a thing like that?'

'Perhaps it was a mix-up,' I suggested, not quite believing it.

'Maybe.' He sighed, still keeping his eyes on the sugary swirls on his plate. 'Anyway it doesn't really matter anymore, as father has decided to sell.'

'What do you mean? Not the Manor surely?'

'I am afraid so.'

'But you can't,' I said, dumbfounded. 'It's been in your family for generations, it's your home...'

'We don't have much choice.'

'What about selling off some of your paintings and things?'

'Selling off the family silver? We have already done a lot of that in the past. Although it may look like we have a lot of expensive paintings, the vast majority are not worth much and, even if we sold the valuable ones, the money we raised would only keep us going for a limited amount of time. We would just be putting off the inevitable.'

I didn't know what to say to him. Both of us sat in silence looking with unseeing eyes at the table between us; our unfinished milkshakes no longer seemed appealing.

Hugo told me that his father had instructed some estate agents who were coming down on Thursday to take photographs and measurements. His father, it seemed, hadn't wasted much time getting things organised.

'Do you fancy going for a ride on Thursday? I can't face being in the house when they are swarming all over the place like ants.'

I said that would be fine, as long as Phil could give me a lift.

We didn't talk about the Manor after that. Hugo

skilfully diverted the conversation to a pair of buzzards he had seen and then gave me a graphic account of their habits and habitat. So I sat and sipped the remains of my milkshake and listened half-heartedly, as my head was full of thoughts about the sale of the Manor. So perhaps the vicar had been right all along.

*

In the end I didn't get Mum a birthday present. After I had left Hugo in the café, I didn't have much time; plus, I had spent some of her birthday present money on my milkshake and doughnut. Hugo had offered to pay but, in the circumstances, I could hardly let him.

In the car on the way home, I kept thinking about the terrible bad luck they had had recently and how hard his father had been trying to turn their fortunes around, in order to not only keep the Manor, but spend some money on it to prevent it deteriorating. Events seemed to conspire against them at every attempt. First the shooting party had been ruined because the shots went missing at the last moment, then the burglary and, finally the private party in tatters because someone had cancelled the caterers. Three things, one after another; what dreadful coincidences. It was all proving too much for Hugo's father. But I couldn't dismiss a nagging little voice which kept repeating: 'There's no such thing as a coincidence, everything happens for a reason.'

*

Cara was taken a back as she read that last sentence because there was that word again. She felt compelled to read on.

31st August

There is, I think, something quite depressing about the end of August. It's probably because the holidays are nearly over and the next one seems such a long way off, but it's more than that. Everything outside looks past its best; blooms have come and gone, the leaves have lost their lustre and vitality, the fields are an almost uniform parchment colour where crops have been harvested, pale stumps being the only reminder that there was ever anything growing there.

As I looked out at the garden and opened my bedroom window, I caught the slight smell of autumn in the cool morning air; a mixture of dampness, mould and decay. The thought of the dark frosty mornings and evenings to come did nothing to lift my mood.

Downstairs, Phil was washing some lettuce and cabbages in the sink. Mum was silently patrolling, noting the mess he was creating in the process but, thankfully, said nothing. Instead she busied herself checking the fridge, as today was shopping day and I was her assistant. Meanwhile, the only sound to be heard was me crunching on some overdone toast.

Supermarket shopping with Mum was not something I looked forward to. Although there were a few compensations. She would usually buy me one or two treats if I went along. I could never decide whether Mum was a really efficient shopper or a bad one, because, by the end of every week there is absolutely nothing left to eat in the house. So she either carefully calculates how much we consume in one week, or else, she simply doesn't buy enough.

Predictably the supermarket was heaving and Mum put me in sole charge of the badly behaved trolley. We had made hardly any progress up the first aisle, when a woman from our village spotted Mum and the two of them stood chatting in the crowded aisle, which was so embarrassing. Mrs Coward is a notorious gossip. As well, I think, as liking the sound of her own voice, she is one of those people who has the knack of being capable of talking fifteen to the dozen, and listening to other people's conversations at the same time. Mum can barely get 'a word in edgeways'. In fact I doubt very much whether Mrs Coward is in the least interested in hearing her opinion. So I steeled myself for a long wait and was about to go off in search of a more interesting aisle, when I heard something which stopped me in my tracks.

'Well who'd have thought it?' Mrs Coward prattled on. 'The Squire must have friends in high places, that's all I can say.'

I thought to myself, *I wish it were!*

'And it's not just a one-off, either,' she continued. 'It seems that it will be a series. I hope we get some well-known actors – like what's-his-name, who was in that Jane Austen film, oh you know who I mean? Anyway, no doubt Jack, at The Dog and Duck will be sprucing up his menus if we are going to be surrounded by a film company – I wonder if they will be looking for any extras?'

What on earth was she talking about? What has Hugo's father to do with a film company? I wish I had paid more attention to the conversation. In the end I couldn't stand it any longer.

'What did you say about the Manor – what's happened?'

'Oh, haven't you heard? The Squire has been offered untold amounts of money by a film company.'

'So he has sold the place quite quickly then,' I said, pleased for Hugo and his father but sad for them at the same time.

'No,' Mrs Coward continued. 'He's not sold it—'

'Rented it out then.'

'No, I was just going on to explain, if you would only care to listen,' Mrs Coward reprimanded, casting an eye at Mum at the same time. 'This film company want to use the Manor for a television series, some historical reproduction, I think that's what she said.'

'Who told you?' I demanded.

'Oh, I have it on good authority. My sister-in-law is Emily Burgess; she rang and told us this morning,' she announced proudly. 'Anyway, I can't stand chatting all day, I'd better get on.'

And with that said, she pushed her trolley forward in a determined manner towards a group of ladies further up the aisle, where she was obviously heading with her exciting news, as well as to catch up with any other village gossip.

We finished our shopping without further distractions and made our way home to an empty house. Phil hadn't yet returned. I helped Mum unpack the shopping, we had lunch and still he wasn't back, which was very frustrating, as I was dying to hear more news from the Manor.

On my way upstairs, I hovered by the telephone in the hall – I just had the feeling it was going to ring, and I knew who it would be. I only had to linger for a few moments, then the phone rang. I grabbed the receiver quickly, resisting the temptation to say: 'Hello Hugo.'

Instead, a familiar voice on the other end said: 'Hello Suzann, it's Hugo.'

Making a pretence of surprise, I replied: 'Oh, hi Hugo, how are things?' I didn't want to let on that I had bumped into the local busybody in the supermarket and had been listening to gossip. It would be too embarrassing.

'Not too bad, actually; it looks like we won't have to sell the Manor after all. We have been approached by a television company. They want to use our house and grounds for a new series. So that's good news.'

'Why! That's fantastic. Hugo. I'm really pleased for you.'

'Yeah, it's a huge relief, I can tell you.

'Actually, I was wondering, instead of coming over on Thursday, if you are not doing anything on Friday afternoon, whether you would like to come around and we could ride over to Beech Farm to have a look at the new foal. You could stay for tea and stay over if you like... Mrs B will be there... It's my birthday, you see and Father thought it would be good to have a friend over? But, don't worry, I'm sure you've probably got something organised, as it's a bit short notice I know. Anyway, I will leave it with you.'

'I would like to come, Hugo,' I said. 'But I will have to check with my mum first. Can I ring you back later?'

We confirmed his number and a time to ring back and hung up. I was doubtful whether Mum would let me sleep over but, to my surprise, she said yes, without any hesitation; whether this was due to the fact that she was busily sorting out a rather large pile of dirty washing, or that she was in a good mood – I'm not sure, but I didn't hang around to wait for her to change her mind and dashed into the hall to ring Hugo back.

Everything was arranged. Mum rang Mrs B to confirm times, whether I needed my sleeping bag or not and to check what present we could buy Hugo. I think Mum was more concerned about that than anything else.

'Just what do you buy a boy who lives in a museum?' she moaned.

TWELVE

The next day Cara and Megan were driven in an official Army car to a services airfield, over an hour's drive away. Before they left, they had said goodbye to Helen, who didn't want to intrude on their reunion.

Once there, they were escorted to a small waiting room which had been set aside for them, where they had a nail-biting wait for her father's flight to land. After what seemed like an eternity to Cara, she saw her father, wearing his characteristic broad grin, supported by crutches, appear in the doorway. He didn't get very far into the room before the two of them rushed at him, nearly knocking him over. The family was reunited again.

*

For the next few days Cara was preoccupied with her dad, she hadn't wanted to let him out of her sight, and was just content to be with him; and because of his injured leg, there were things he needed help with. There was a lot to catch up on too; of course he couldn't talk too much about his mission, though this pleased Cara in a way, as she didn't really want to know. It would be a reminder that things could all so easily have turned out very differently.

*

One evening a few days later, when her mum and dad had gone round to a friend's for a meal, Cara remembered Suzann's diary, which she hadn't finished reading. Upstairs in her attic bedroom, she picked it up again and continued where she had left off.

2nd September

I don't go to stay at many people's houses, so I was looking forward to staying at the Manor.

I woke with a sensation of excitement and anticipation when I realised what day it was. This was accompanied by a feeling of something else which I couldn't quite make sense of, so I dismissed it and concentrated on checking that I had packed everything I wanted to take with me.

The morning seemed to drag a bit; Mum had a little job to perform at the vicarage, which meant that I was left on my own for a couple of hours with not much to do.

Phil had asked me to water his tubs so I wandered into the back garden. Surveying Phil's tidy and well-organised patch, which despite many plants being past their best, still managed to resemble a garden that would rival anyone else's in the village, I thought, not for the first time, what a paradox Phil was. Inside the house he was very untidy, disorganised sometimes, and occasionally even clumsy but, once outside, it was as if he underwent some kind of transformation, as he becomes the complete opposite.

I found the watering can, by the neatly wound-up hose pipe next to the greenhouse, and set about watering the tubs along the fence when I noticed someone out of the corner of my eye in next door's garden. Looking up, I recognise the figure straight away. It was Archie, sitting on a wooden bench, looking out at his neglected garden, which had once been his pride and joy. He used to joke about Phil being his rival at the local vegetable show, but I don't think he took it quite that seriously – unlike Phil. It was sad to see him now sat amongst the towering weeds and untidy ill-defined flower beds, he was obviously deep in thought, I wasn't sure he had even seen me.

'Hello Archie,' I shouted over the fence.

Turning his head in my direction, he did his best to hide the tortured look of the recently bereaved.

'Hello pet. Phil got you working, has he?'

'Yes.' I smiled back.

After that, I could sense that he wasn't too keen to converse any further, as he turned his head away, reverting to contemplating his dishevelled plot, so I resumed my watering.

As I was replacing the watering can in its allotted position, I caught sight of him again just sitting there only this time; I was relieved to see he was not alone. Sat next to him was Maud and it was she who looked over in my direction and smiled as I passed near to them. How I wished I could tell him, but I knew he would think like everyone else, that I was stark raving bonkers.

Phil came back at lunch time and, after a quick bite to eat, we were soon driving past the derelict gatekeeper's lodge and bumping along, Phil doing his best to avoid the worst of the potholes in the dusty track hedged by rhododendrons, the branches of which almost touched the car as it made its perilous journey to the Manor.

Hugo met us at the back door and took my bags from Phil, making some joke about the amount of stuff I had brought, which was a bit embarrassing as I was a bit self-conscious about the lack of a smart or fashionable overnight bag like those I had seen some of the girls bring into school, when they were obviously staying over somewhere. I also had a couple of carrier bags for my riding things, so I could have done without Hugo's little 'joke'.

Hugo's manners only extended to the scullery, where he dropped my bags, saying that we would get them later. Was he too embarrassed to bring them any further into the house?

'Are you hungry?' he asked, reaching into a large cake tin.

'No, thank you,' I replied watching him fish out a handful of biscuits which he proceeded to demolish in quick succession.

'Come on, I'll show you where you will be staying.'

He led the way into the hall, up the staircase to the gallery and past the now familiar family portraits looking disdainfully down at me, as though I had no right to be in the house. *They're probably right*, I thought to myself, thinking about my paltry assortment of bags lying in the scullery. Being a bit self-absorbed as I made my way along the long galleried landing, I didn't notice her until we were almost level, then I stopped abruptly, whilst Hugo continued to walk ahead. She looked altered and this wasn't just due to the fact that she was wearing a different dress of pale lilac, in a style that wasn't quite so full as before; her hair was tied up this time in a fairly elaborate way; she looked older, in her late twenties or early thirties perhaps.

She half smiled at me, then turned and pointed in the direction of the portrait and her expression changed to one of seriousness:

'Look carefully at the portrait,' she turned and said to me. 'It's not what it appears to be.'

'What's wrong with it?' I replied.

I didn't get the answer I was hoping for, as Hugo spun round and asked me what I was talking about. I could feel my face colouring, as I racked my brains for some believable explanation or some witty comment, but words failed me, all I could mutter was: 'No one, just myself.' Hugo obviously wasn't convinced as he continued to stare at me.

Please don't let him think I'm some nutter, I thought to myself.

'Do you often talk to yourself?'

'Being an only child, I do it all the time,' I said, a little more confidently. 'Don't you?'

'No, I don't,' Hugo said, but by now I was walking ahead of him so he could not see my beetroot-coloured face.

I never have been a good liar; Mum can always tell when I am not telling the truth: 'It's written all over your face,' she would say.

Hugo led me to the far end of the house, into a corridor I hadn't seen before. At the end of it, we turned left into a lovely big room, with two enormous windows overlooking the lawns at the back of the house and views of the surrounding countryside. Each of the windows had window seats beneath, complete with burgundy-coloured cushions. Although they were somewhat faded, they still looked posh to me. The centrepiece of the room was a beautiful big bed. Behind the headboard, velvet curtains hung, which matched the window seat cushions. They were gathered and tied back at each side with large tasselled cords.

'What a lovely room,' I said, looking around and trying my best to sound not too over-awed but, at the same time, realising that you could probably fit the whole of our downstairs into this one room.

'Mrs B is just opposite,' he said, pointing vaguely at the door. 'And my room is just up the stairs, round the corner. The bathroom is next door but one. Hope you don't mind sharing with Mrs B?'

At home I have to share with two others, so it was hardly going to be a problem, I assured him.

'Anyway, shall we go for a ride? I will give you a hand with the rest of your things.'

'No, it's fine, I can manage, thank you.'

'Right then, I had better go and change. See you downstairs in twenty minutes then?'

*

On my way down to the kitchen to collect the rest of my bags, I passed the portrait that Carlotta had been so keen for me to look at. As there was no one about, I peered at it closely and carefully, so much so that I could smell its musty scent and see the brush strokes on the canvas.

'What on earth am I supposed to be looking for?' I

wondered.

'You obviously like that painting, don't you dear?' I heard Mrs B's voice from the hall below and, not for the first time that afternoon, I felt my face colouring – pure beetroot. What must I look like with my nose practically glued to an old painting!

'Er... yes, it's lovely... I quite like art,' I lied. 'I was just looking at the brush techniques.' Where that came from I don't know. I almost believed it myself, it sounded quite genuine!

'Don't ask me, dear. The Squire is the one to talk to if you are interested in art. Now, Hugo tells me that you two are off riding. Well, just make sure you are back for tea at 5.30, as I am making Hugo's favourite. See you later.'

The problem with this place is that it is just too big. At our house you get plenty of warning before someone is about to come into a room as you can hear them. Here they see you long before you hear them coming.

Fifteen minutes later, I met up with Hugo and we made our way to the stables where both our horses had been saddled and were ready to go.

'I did this earlier to save time,' Hugo admitted.

I stroked Flame's forelock gently and produced a couple of carrots I had found lying around in our kitchen, some of Phil's specialities – organic too!

Outside in the stable yard, I looked up and saw a few darker clouds to our left and hoped that they were moving away from us, as I hadn't brought anything waterproof with me.

We headed for the now familiar bridle path and broke into a canter. When we reached the fields at the end of the path, Hugo broke into a gallop, I did my best to catch up with him but found it difficult and he was too far in front to hear me shouting at him to slow down. Thankfully the ground started to rise slightly and he gradually slowed to a walking pace, allowing me a chance to catch up.

'Do you know where we are?' Hugo asked when I had drawn level with him.

I looked around at the gently undulating landscape, dotted with clumps of trees. Ahead, there was what looked like a wooded area, but it didn't seem familiar. I was sure he hadn't brought me out this way before.

I told him that I had no idea where we were, because we had been going at such a 'break-neck speed' that the only thing on my mind was keeping my seat.

'So, forgive me, if I haven't taken much notice of the countryside!' I said, trying to get my breath back.

Hugo apologised for going too fast, but I think he was secretly pleased that I didn't recognise the place. I sensed it was to be a surprise.

'This is Finglebury Ring, the site of an ancient Bronze Age settlement. We've had archaeologists and historians investigating it over the years; they even made a TV programme about it a few years ago. Come on, let's tie the horses up and walk into the centre.'

We dismounted and tied the horses to a wooden fence post and made our way onto the ring, a big mound which I presumed must be circular. Ahead, in the centre, was a fairly dense wood, which I must admit didn't look too inviting.

Hugo took the lead and proceeded to give me a short history lesson, explaining how the Romans had attacked it in AD 64 and built a road nearby, the outline of which we would be able to see from the other side of the mound. We were, by now, some way in toward the centre, our progress being slowed by overgrown shrubs and brambles, which attached themselves to our clothes. I was so glad I hadn't worn shorts.

The bushes looked to be getting closer and closer and I was beginning to feel uncomfortable, as we had to pick our way carefully to avoid getting slashed by barbs. Tall stinging nettles brushed against my jeans, catching my left arm in the process but, worst of all, was the feeling of panic I felt beginning to rise up inside. That, and the sick feeling in the pit of my stomach, told me that bad things had happened here, even though it was a long, long time ago. The bad energy still hung around like a dark web, waiting to trap those sensitive enough to feel it. More than anything I just wanted to turn and run, but I stubbornly tried to push the dark images that were rapidly filling my head out of my thoughts. I avoided looking at anything but Hugo's back, which was frequently obscured by the dark branches. It seemed as if they were grabbing at him like hungry fingers reaching for a tempting morsel.

After what seemed like ages but was probably only minutes, we suddenly came to a clearing, which should have been a relief. There were no trees or shrubs; just ferns and longish grass obscuring our feet. In the centre stood a large standing stone protruding from the ground at a slight angle. Hugo was already walking towards it but I just couldn't move any closer, my head now bursting with the effort to control the dreadful images which were trying to fight their way into my mind.

Hugo walked up to touch the stone.

'Do you know what this is?' he asked, running his hand over the rough contours of the stone.

I wanted to shout at him, 'I know, I know.'

'This marks the spot where the gibbet stood. This was known as "Hangman's Hill". For centuries they used to hang people here, in this very spot,' he said, turning to look at me but, I didn't hear what he had to say next, as I had my hands over my ears to shut out the noise of the shouting and cries. I could no longer stop the horrible images of people lined up waiting for the hangman's noose. I had to get out of there.

I turned and ran in the direction we came from, no longer caring about the branches and brambles closing around me, tearing at my T-shirt and scratching my arms; the feeling of blind fear drove me on.

Eventually, I reached the end of the wood and found myself on the edge of the ditch separating the inner and outer rings; I ran down it and up the other side. As I did, my foot caught in a rabbit hole and I fell over on my side so that I rolled over and over, finally coming to a halt at the bottom. I lay there gasping for breath, tears pricking my eyes and a burning pain in my ankle but, at least, the voices and the fear were behind me.

I am not too sure how long I lay there watching a buzzard circling high above in the late afternoon sky. Then I became aware of a voice calling my name; it was Hugo. The feelings of panic now were replaced by those of embarrassment; what must he think? I must look so stupid. How could I explain this one? Goodness knows what I must have looked like; my hair must have resembled an orange haystack. It had long ago escaped its hair clips and bands that had been carefully arranged earlier. Running a hand through it, I felt there was certainly enough grass in it and goodness knows what else.

'Suzann!' I heard his breathless call. 'Suzann, Suzann!' Each time sounding increasingly more anxious.

At this point, I was sufficiently recovered to reveal my whereabouts. Wiping the last of my tears away, I sat up gingerly, feeling a slight pulling on my ankle as I did. I turned to see Hugo, not too far away, running over in my direction with a distinctly worried look on his face.

'Are you alright?' he asked, looking concerned.

'I've hurt my ankle,' I said, trying to sound as normal as possible.

'Can you walk on it?'

'I don't know,' I said, trying to get up. Hugo held out his hand for me to grasp for support whilst I heaved myself upright; it evidently wasn't broken, as I was able to stand but it hurt quite a bit when I tried to put my full weight on it. So I hobbled about like this for a few minutes, holding onto Hugo's arm, whilst we assessed the damage.

'How's that? Does it feel any better?'

'I'm OK,' I said. I didn't want to make a fuss.

'I'm really sorry,' he said quietly. 'I didn't mean to scare you bringing you here, I thought you would be interested that's all.'

'What, in hanging?'

'No, in the history of the place – you told me you were keen on history and this place is crammed with it.'

No kidding, I thought to myself.

'This place isn't even open to the public, because it's on our land, so I thought you would like to see it,' he continued quite seriously. 'Your own private viewing,' he added with a wry smile.

'You wait here whilst I get the horses.' Like I was capable of doing anything else. 'I won't be long.'

Hugo obviously thought I ran off because I was scared; he's no idea how much, though this was not down to the dark wood or the thought of the hangman. The images I saw and the feelings that went with them were terrifying.

'Do you think you will be ok riding?' Hugo appeared, leading both our horses.

I hobbled towards Flame.

'I think I will need a bit of help,' I said, sounding too pathetically feeble for my liking.

Hugo gave me a leg-up, which wasn't easy as we had to avoid hurting my ankle. To my relief though, it didn't feel too bad once I had my foot in the stirrup.

'Don't worry, we will take it very easy on the way back,' Hugo assured me.

This is why it took quite a long time to retrace our steps back to the Manor. Hugo, meanwhile, kept up a cheerful chatter about the house and his father's plans for improvement, once the contract had been drawn up with the film company. Apparently, a television company had been on the lookout for a suitable location to film the historical television series for some time. The producer had been at the disastrous dinner party at the Manor a couple of weeks ago and had decided that it would be ideal. I was pleased something good had come out of that evening. When they are not filming, Hugo's father plans to open the house and grounds to the public, as well as having a small souvenir shop selling a range of items connected with the television programme. I told Hugo how relieved I felt for them that they no longer had to sell their home.

For my part, I was just grateful that he didn't make any further reference to my hasty exit, and the more distance between Finglebury Rings and us, the better I felt.

*

On our return, we met Mrs B outside in the stable yard.

'Ah, there you are, I was beginning to wonder where you two were as it's nearly tea time. Where did you get to? Did you have a good ride?'

'We went as far as Finglebury Rings, but Suzann

took a bit of a tumble and I'm afraid she may have sprained her ankle,' Hugo said as he quickly dismounted and then moved around to help me.

I carefully swung my injured foot over Flame's withers and slid down to where Hugo caught me and then gently lowered me to the ground. With his arm around my waist to support me, we made our way towards the scullery, with Mrs B, who was already fusing about ice, bandages and even calling the doctor, leading the way.

'No, really, Mrs B,' I tried to assure her. 'I'm fine, it's just a bit bruised, that's all. I will be fine once I've had a bit of a rest.'

'Well, we'll see shall we, once I've had a look at it? Now sit down and take your shoe off, whilst I inspect the damage.'

I loosened my laces and gingerly removed my shoe. It didn't feel too bad now, in fact there wasn't any visible sign that anything was wrong. Mrs B disappeared for a few minutes and returned waving a bag of frozen peas.

'This will do the trick,' she said triumphantly, promptly thrusting the wet bag onto my ankle. 'Just keep that there, whilst I finish off your tea.'

I looked over at Hugo, who was looking at my ankle rather sheepishly, and I remembered the reason why I had been invited over – it was Hugo's birthday. I began to feel a bit guilty that I had ruined it for him.

'It's OK Hugo, honestly, I'm feeling a bit better now.' I lied, but his face visibly brightened. Not only was I feeling guilty but a bit stupid as well. What must he think of me rushing out of Finglebury Ring so dramatically? Of course he wouldn't understand what I had experienced there, he would only have seen me overreacting and racing off at top speed, like a frightened rabbit and performing some kind of amateur acrobatics for my grand finale. Perhaps he thinks I am a bit of an attention-seeker? Oh, my god! I felt my face colouring at the very thought of it, and at that moment, I just wanted to go home – but to ask would seem rude and be even more embarrassing.

Hugo left me in the kitchen to go and change out of his riding gear. I was left with a damp bag of peas plastered to my ankle, which already felt numb with the cold. Mrs B was busily putting the finishing touches to Hugo's birthday cake, which looked like chocolate. Making the most of some time to myself to calm down, I tried to test out my ankle by walking. To my relief, it seemed a lot better, as I managed to walk a few steps without any pain. It just felt a bit stiff. Perhaps it was just a bruise after all.

*

After a lovely tea of lasagne, salad and garlic bread, Hugo suggested that we watch a film, which was a good idea in view of my ankle although, by now, it was feeling much better, no doubt helped by the neat bandage Mrs B had insisted upon me wearing. Hugo drew the curtains in the sitting room and dimmed the lights. The film was a crime thriller and he made a point of asking whether I would be alright watching it, as it was a bit scary in parts. He really must think I am some sort of wimp, especially after this afternoon. I was just glad the lights were low and he couldn't see my bright red face!

*

Later, I lay in the large, burgundy bed, which felt surprisingly comfortable, despite its age. I looked around the bedroom with its antique furniture, illuminated only by the small bedside light which cast a soft and forgiving glow over everything it touched, erasing the years of neglect and the damage done by the passage of time. I found it difficult to sleep; my mind felt strangely alert as though in anticipation of some unknown event. I kept thinking about what had happened that day, although I tried to block out the dreadful scenes at Finglebury Rings.

I must have dozed for a little while, then tossed and turned, my active mind denying my now tired body the sleep it needed.

After a while I got out of bed to open the window a little further; it was still warm and the night air smelt sweet and fresh. Somewhere in the distance an owl screeched just as a full moon was beginning to emerge from behind a cloud, hanging like a giant lantern in the sky and revealing a mysterious landscape below my window, bathed in a silvery light so bright that the trees and shrubs cast shadows.

I was just about to return to bed, when some movement caught my eye towards the opposite end of the house. It was difficult to make out what it was, so I waited and watched but the brilliant moon slipped behind a cloud, shrouding the whole scene in darkness once again. Deciding it was probably a fox, I closed the curtains and tried to sleep.

This time sleep came more easily, although not for long as I became aware of a voice calling my name, at first easy to ignore as it seemed like a dream, but gradually the voice grew louder and more persistent.

'Suzann, Suzann,' the voice repeated.

'Leave me alone,' I answered, exasperated to be woken.

But the voice continued.

'Suzann.'

'Go away.' The voice wouldn't be silenced even with the covers over my head, there was no escape and by now I was awake and angry.

'Why can't you leave me alone?' Opening my eyes and raising myself up slightly, I could make out the unmistakable figure of Carlotta, although now much older, probably in her forties, standing at the foot of my bed.

'What do you want?' I almost shouted at her.

She told me to get up and follow her.

'No, please, I'm tired,' I pleaded, in vain.

Wearily, I dragged myself out of my warm cocoon, hastily pulled on a pair of socks and a T-shirt over my pyjamas – just in case – as I had no idea where she was taking me. Thankfully, my ankle seemed almost back to normal, I felt only a slight twinge as I put my sock over Mrs B's more than ample bandage.

I stepped out in the corridor, leaving my door open to give some light to see by. Carlotta was by now turning left past the stairs that led to Hugo's room, where she disappeared from view. As I stumbled forward, I stubbed my toe on the corner of the hall table, I couldn't help but whisper a slight gasp as it hurt, and the old floor boards creaked and groaned under my weight. Ahead lay another corridor with a window in the middle which admitted a pale light partly illuminating the empty passageway. Where had she gone?

I stood leaning against the wall rubbing my toe and waiting for some sign, when I thought I heard a noise, it could have been a creaking floor board, or a water pipe – I wasn't sure. Just then, I felt a presence behind me; all too quickly a hand covered my mouth and another wrapped around my waist. In terror I tried to turn around, just as a voice said: 'Don't scream, you'll wake Mrs B.' The hand over my mouth was released, and swinging round, I launched into an attack on Hugo who was smiling whilst trying to dodge my flying fist.

'What on earth are you doing creeping up on me like that?' I whispered angrily.

'I was just about to ask you what you think you are

doing creeping around my house in the middle of the night.'

His question was enough to stop my strikes at him. Just how do I explain what I am doing here in the middle of the night?

'I thought I heard something,' I offered, which wasn't quite a lie.

Hugo looked at me as though he suspected I was keeping something from him.

'Like what?'

'I'm not sure, but it sounded as though it was coming from down here,' I said, pointing towards the end of the corridor, where it turned to the right.

I started to walk toward the end, feeling sure that Carlotta had disappeared around the corner.

'Suzann, wait! What sort of noise was it?'

Despite the slight ache in my ankle I managed to get to the bottom before Hugo, just in time to see Carlotta disappear through a doorway towards the end of this second hallway.

'Do you know where you are going?'

'I'm not sure,' was all I could come up with in reply, hesitating by the slightly open door I had seen her go through and peering into the darkness.

'Well thankfully, I do. This leads to the disused part of the house and, lucky for you; I came prepared for a late-night exploration.'

Suddenly, the way forward was illuminated by a beam of light from a torch which Hugo was holding.

'Here, you might as well take it, as you seem to be the one who knows where you want to go. Although, if you really wanted to see this part of the house, you only had to ask.'

I shone the torch; ahead a narrow flight of stone steps curved around to the right in a tight spiral.

'After you!' Hugo said with a slight hint of sarcasm.

The stone felt cold under my socks as we slowly made our way up, our ascent made even more difficult as there was no hand rail. My left hand skimmed the cold dusty wall, which was probably full of spiders, but I tried not to look, concentrating instead on holding the torch so we both could see where we were putting our feet. The door was open slightly and, as I pushed it with my free hand, I could see a large room with three large windows to the right, each with a window seat underneath. The room was empty, except for a couple of old chairs, a rocking horse with one leg missing and a few boxes. I then recognised it as the room I had been in when I saw the old man.

I didn't see Carlotta straight away; it was only as I turned around that I spotted her standing by the door, pointing towards the back of one of the chairs.

'What can you see, Suzann?' Hugo asked, glancing around the room. 'Tell me.'

Somehow I knew he wasn't simply talking about the boxes and the old rocking horse.

'I'm not sure,' I said, looking back at the fireplace which now had a roaring fire burning in the grate. As I walked slowly towards it, I could hear the crackle and spitting of the wood as it burned. In front of the fireplace stood a large wing-backed leather chair, and, from where I was standing, I could see a matching leather footstool upon which rested the legs of a man.

Instinctively, I knew it was the man I had seen here before, I could feel the air heavy with his sorrow and, as I approached him, I could feel this even more keenly.

Sitting down opposite him, on the other chair, I looked at him slumped in his chair, still clutching the photograph I had seen him with and I began to see images of his life form in front of me.

First, I see a happy young family; the man sitting in front of me looks so different as a young man and with him is Carlotta. Both look happy. They have two small sons; I see them playing together, climbing trees, play-fighting and causing mischief. I hear the man calling them Max and Edmund. The next image I see is when they are older. Edmund, is shown as being more confident and outgoing than Max, who is a bit of a loner. As they grow into men, Max goes off to Oxford University, leaving Edmund at home where he soon becomes known as a bit of a ladies' man, soon earning a reputation for breaking the hearts of countless ladies across the county. Much to his father's dismay, he starts to drink heavily and then gets involved with gambling, soon running up huge debts which he expects his father to pay off.

I see angry scenes between Edmund and his father Ralph. He is trying to get him to focus on his responsibilities as heir to the Manor. He tells him that his patience is running out and he is no longer prepared to bail him out every time he gets himself into debt. His words appear to fall on deaf ears, as the next image I see is Edmund becoming involved with a serious scandal as well as running up massive debts which his father is forced to settle for him. After that I see him sending Edmund away to Italy, where his father believes he will 'learn the error of his ways', but Edmund has other ideas. He marries a local girl without telling his parents and arrives back home with her. At first, his father believes that Edmund has possibly changed and lets him take on more of the running of the estate. This turns out to be a big mistake as he and his wife spend lavishly and his gambling debts mount. Ralph watches, with great sadness and dismay, the way Edmund and his wife conduct themselves. It breaks his heart to see the estate, which he had worked so hard to maintain, being bled dry; even some of their farms and cottages have to be sold in order to fund their extravagant lifestyle. In the end, Ralph decides to take drastic action. In order to save the Manor, he makes the painful decision to disinherit Edmund, sending him and his wife back to Italy. Max is then made the sole heir and takes over the running of the estate. This all takes its toll on Carlotta, who is devoted to both her sons but has a special bond with Edmund. I see that she is heartbroken at his banishment and never fully recovers from it. Nor does it seem that she really forgives her husband for banishing her favourite son. Distancing herself from him and their life together, she eventually slips quietly away from the earthly life one night, leaving Ralph a broken man.

The images gradually cleared, revealing Ralph as an old man consumed with sadness. I looked back at Carlotta who was still standing by the door and, suddenly, I understood the reason why she had been pestering me and why she had brought me to this room. She couldn't reach her husband because he couldn't forgive himself. Looking at her, I could feel the strong feelings of love and forgiveness she felt for him. I decided I must try to speak to him.

Sitting on the edge of the chair opposite him and leaning forward to look into the old man's tragic face, I whispered his name gently:

'Ralph.'

He didn't even look up from the worn photograph he was still holding.

'Ralph,' I repeated a bit louder.

Still no response. Perhaps he can't hear me, maybe I can't talk to every spirit I see. I began to doubt my own abilities. I looked towards Carlotta, who was sending me powerful images of the two of them together, laughing.

'Do you know that your wife still loves you?'

Sill nothing.

'I know that because she told me, in fact she is here now standing by the door.'

Slowly he lifted his eyes from the mauled photograph and looked at me. So he can hear me, I haven't lost my touch after all.

'She says that you must learn to forgive yourself, the way she has forgiven you.'

I could sense that he was struggling with this part; like, about eighty years of struggle. How on earth was I going to make a difference? I needed some help. I looked towards Carlotta again and she sent me a different image of the two of them having a heated argument after Edmund had been sent away. She was very upset and angry as she missed her son. Ralph had said: 'If you miss him that much, why don't you pack your bags and move to Italy with him?'

When I repeated this to Ralph, tears welled up in his eyes.

'There is nothing anyone can do to change the

past, all you can do is learn to accept and forgive. That is what Carlotta has done and she is asking you to do the same. Only when you have done that can you two be together and she is waiting for you over here by the door.'

Ralph slowly raised himself to his feet and turns around to look towards the door, where Carlotta was standing. I could feel the depth of emotion between them. He looked at first as though he could not see her, then gradually his face changes and softens, his eyes widen and his whole face radiates pure joy, as he made his way towards the door and Carlotta. Once they are reunited, both are engulfed in a white light, so bright, I had to look away for a few moments. When I looked back, the light was much smaller, resembling a shrinking balloon someone had let the air escape from until eventually, it was no bigger than a ping pong ball. It floated around the room towards me and around me and then finally disappeared.

I sat down on the dusty chair, feeling suddenly exhausted. The once dark room was turning a pale greyish-pink as the sun was beginning to rise, eating into the darkness.

Turning to look at the window, I suddenly caught sight of Hugo, whom I had completely forgotten about, sitting on an old wooden crate. Thankfully, I couldn't see the expression on his face – I could only guess!

'Are you OK?' I asked nervously.

'I'm not sure,' came an uncertain response. 'I always thought you were a bit different, now I know why.'

'What did you see?'

'Nothing much, I can sometimes sense things but, what went on here was different. Tell me what happened.'

'What did you hear?'

'You talking to someone. Who was it?'

'Well, let's say that I don't think you will be seeing the lady in white anymore, who, by the way, didn't wear a white dress. Anyway, I'm tired. It's late and I want some sleep,' I said, rising to my feet and making my way out of the room.

'Yeah, but you can't just disappear off to bed without telling me what happened back there and don't try and make out that nothing did – 'cause I saw things too.'

'Later, Hugo, I'm just too tired.'

Hugo followed me as we made our way down the

spiral staircase and along the bare corridors, although he was still asking questions:

'So what did the lady in blue, pink want?'

'I'll tell you in the morning, Hugo. It's too late now.'

'But it already is morning.'

We must have taken a wrong turning somewhere, as we had emerged on to the galleried landing. As we passed the portraits of Hugo's ancestors, some of whom looked disdainfully down at us as we passed. All of a sudden I heard Lady Carlotta's voice:

'This picture is not what it seems, Suzann.'

'You keep saying that, but I don't understand what you mean.'

'What don't you understand...?' Hugo stopped mid-sentence and raised his eyes to the ceiling, then continued as though talking to himself. '...Oh, here we go again!'

'Look behind the smile,' she said, her voice gradually trailing away.

Suddenly I knew exactly what she meant.

'Hugo, I know this may sound strange...'

'After tonight, nothing you say can ever sound strange!'

Is this picture worth much?'

'It's not by any notable artist, why?'

'Just a hunch!'

'Oh yeah!' he said sarcastically.

'Can you go and get a sharp knife from the kitchen for me?'

He didn't ask why, just looked at me quizzically for a couple of seconds, then ran down the stairs into the hall. Looking back at the picture, I thought: *I hope you're right about this, Carlotta.*

Hearing a noise in the hall below, I turned expecting to see Hugo, but looking over the banisters, there wasn't much to see as it still wasn't quite light enough. Then I saw his dark shape making his way from the kitchen, bounding up the stairs. As he handed me the small vegetable knife, he said: 'I hope you know what you are doing, Suz!'

The knife was sharp and I cut very carefully a small line at the corner of the picture where it joined the frame.

It will be easier to repair, I thought to myself.

Although the knife was sharp, it was difficult to cut through the tough canvass, hardened by age.

After several attempts cutting along the same line, I could see that I had been successful. Sliding the knife underneath the canvas, I held my breath as I lifted it. This could be the most expensive mistake I could ever make if I was wrong.

The canvas lifted with little resistance but, I couldn't easily see what, if anything lay underneath.

'Pass me the torch, will you?' I asked Hugo, trying to conceal my anxiety.

The torch shone a bright beam of light into the dark space I had revealed and something shiny reflected back.

'What can you see? Is there another painting underneath?'

'I'm not sure,' I replied honestly. 'I will have to lift a bit more of the painting.'

Turning, I looked at Hugo for a sign that it would be ok.

'Go on, then, I'll hold the torch.'

I resumed my careful carving, only just aware of a slight noise in the hall below as I did so.

The cutting was made easier this time as I knew just how much force to apply.

'OK, this should do it,' I announced, my heart beating so loudly I was sure Hugo would hear it.

I slowly lifted the canvas and for a few seconds we looked at the space underneath. The light of the torch revealed a surface which was definitely painted with rich browns, reds and greens.

'Oh, my god!' I heard Hugo exclaim. Then after a few moments, 'Let's cut through the last bit so we can get a better look, this looks a bit special.'

Hugo took the knife from me and with far less care than I had shown, cut down both sides of the painting as far as he could reach. Silently he pushed the top portrait aside to reveal the full glory of the sight beneath it.

I heard Hugo inhale audibly, as he surveyed the beautiful landscape painting, shining his torch on rolling hills flowing down to a river where a group of people stood by the water's edge, under a large oak tree. His eyes seemed to grow larger by the second, as he scanned the picture.

'I don't believe this,' he exclaimed. 'Look!'

I followed his outstretched finger, which was pointing towards the bottom right-hand corner.

'What?' I asked, noting nothing of particular

interest in that part of the picture.

'The signature – what does it say?'

He shone the torch and I struggled to make out the name 'Constable.'

Silently we both turned to look at each other, Hugo's eyes as wide as saucers just then the clock in the hall began to chime. It was four-thirty and daylight was now beginning to seep into the great hall.

It was then that I noticed a figure making its way up the stairs towards us.

'Well, well. Congratulations on your find, dear boy.'

Hugo spun around to face Doctor Fitzgerald.

'Now this is very convenient, I must say. No one knows about this little beauty, do they?' he said, lifting the picture of Lady Carlotta and glancing at the newly found painting, and carefully scrutinising the signature of the artist.

'I presume this is genuine.'

'What are you doing here?' Hugo asked, suddenly finding his voice.

'Good question – and you shall have your answer - all in good time,' the doctor replied. 'But first let's get this little beauty down.'

He then lifted the large painting down from its hook on the wall, resting it against the wall, where he then proceeded to rip the original from the frame.

'What do you think you are doing?' Hugo said, making a move to stop him.

The doctor pushed him forcefully so that Hugo fell backwards onto the floor.

Visibly stunned, he got up and again attempted to stop the doctor.

'Don't be stupid, boy,' he said, turning quickly and bringing out a gun from his jacket pocket. 'Over there, both of you, against the wall where I can see you,' he ordered roughly, waving his gun in the direction of the top of the stairs.

He continued to rip the last bits of Lady Carlotta's picture from the frame, tossing it carelessly to one side, as we both watched in fear and bewilderment.

'What is it you want?' Hugo demanded, sounding braver than I thought he would be feeling right now.

'Oh, I've got more than I came here for, dear boy,' the doctor replied with a strange satisfied look on his face. 'But it's no more than I deserve.'

At this stage I admit to having grave feelings of

foreboding. As I looked across at Hugo I think he too felt that we could be in danger. Slowly he reached for the torch which was near to his right hand; once he had secured it, he quickly hid it up his sleeve.

As if sensing movement, Doctor Fitzgerald turned his attention away from cutting out the newly discovered picture from its frame. Looking at Hugo and me, his facial expression changed into a menacing glare.

'Now, what to do with you two?' the doctor said, deliberately taking his time to emphasise that he was in charge, at the same time hitting his gun rhythmically into the palm of his hand.

'Right, on your feet, slowly, no sudden movements and don't try anything silly or you will get hurt,' he said as he quickly rolled up the newly discovered landscape painting.

I was feeling so scared by now that I doubted whether I would be able to stand.

The doctor stood slightly to the side, as we both stood.

'Off you go.' He pointed in the direction of the main stairs. 'Slowly now.'

I followed Hugo to the top of the stairs, my legs

shaking like jelly so that I had to hold onto the banister to steady myself. I noticed Hugo in front of me do the same. We were about halfway down when I saw Hugo, who was closer to the banister than I was, gently release the torch he had been hiding up his sleeve. This provided the diversion he had been hoping for as it hit the large wooden chest in the hall and clattered along the marble floor. Hugo didn't hesitate for a second, unlike the doctor, who I sensed was startled momentarily. He had the picture in one hand and his gun in the other, which gave us a bit of a head start. Hugo grabbed my hand and we ran down the remaining stairs and into the hall, as fast as we could.

From the hall we ran down to the dining room; had we not been pursued by the mad doctor, I would have asked Hugo why we were running deeper into the house. But the doctor was hot on our heels as we ran into the dining room and closed the door. There was no key, and we ran to the door at the other end. We were luckier with this one; the key was in the lock so Hugo quickly locked it, just in time to hear the doctor trying to open it.

Hugo again grabbed my hand and we continued running towards what I was able to recognise as the door to the study; it was open. Once inside, he led me to the bookcase. As he lifted the right book, the bookcase opened up to reveal its secret.

'Quickly,' Hugo whispered as we both stepped inside the dark interior.

As the bookcase closed silently behind us, we heard the door to the study being flung open. Not moving a muscle, hardly daring to breathe, we listened in the darkness as the doctor moved around the room. After what seemed like an eternity, there was no more noise. Hugo decided it was safe to move and silently taking my hand, he led us into the pitch-black tunnel.

We stumbled blindly on, Hugo still clutching my hand (or was it me who clung to his?), one arm stretched out to the side wall, our only guide. The stones felt rough, although I barely noticed when my fingers caught sharp edges, as we inched our way forward. My fear almost palpable, even the sound of my own breathing seemed to come from somewhere else. It was as though we had slipped into another dimension, time became distorted. I had no idea how long we had been down there; minutes passed, but felt like hours.

At some stage I caught my already injured foot on

something hard and felt myself falling until I hit the wall of the tunnel. It hurt, but I was barely aware of the throbbing pain as I worried about whether the noise I had created would enable the doctor to locate us. I wanted to cry. I wanted my mum. I wanted to get out of this terrible darkness.

As Hugo helped me to my feet, he whispered so quietly I could hardly hear him: 'Are you alright?'

'Yes,' I managed to whisper in reply.

After a while Hugo came to an abrupt stop and let go of my hand. I could hear him running his hands over the stone walls.

'We're at the scullery door,' he announced quietly.

There was a soft clicking sound followed by a blinding shaft of light as Hugo opened the door a fraction, it was then we heard the voices.

'Victor!'

The female voice sound familiar but I couldn't quite place it.

'Well,' the voice continued. 'Where are they? Don't tell me you've lost them. You fool.'

'I've searched all the downstairs rooms; they must be hiding somewhere. But we've got the painting, so we might as well forget about them and get out of here.'

'Oh yes! And how far would we get before those two calls the police? We have to find them.'

I recognised who the voice; it was the doctor's wife, although she didn't sound quite as genteel as she usually did.

My fear seemed to have soared to a new level; I wasn't sure whether the distant knocking noise I could hear was the sound of my knees knocking or my teeth chattering. I wondered what on earth we were going to do.

We waited in silence, hardly daring to breathe, then, after we had not heard any further sound from the scullery, Hugo whispered:

'We could probably make a run for it now. They're no doubt searching another part of the house. Wait here whilst I check the coast is clear.'

There was a slight scraping noise as Hugo opened the door wide enough for him to poke his head through. The light was so bright after the darkness of the tunnel that I had to momentarily close my eyes. When I opened them again I saw part of the scullery in front of us. Hugo waited as we both listened.

'Come on, we'll make a run for the back door,' he whispered.

We eased ourselves out from the opening which was disguised as the door to an old cupboard. Although my eyes hadn't fully adjusted to the brightness of the daylight, I could make out the door to the outside and freedom to our left.

Hugo grabbed my arm and we quickly made a dash for the back door. He pushed down on the ancient looking handle; it creaked and groaned but the door didn't move. Hugo tried again and again in desperation but, it was clear, it was locked.

'Where's the key?' I asked in sheer panic.

'Is this what you are looking for?' Mrs Fitzgerald's steely voice was heard asking.

We both turned around to see her and the doctor standing in the doorway to the scullery, barring any possible means of escape. Her face was twisted into a sardonic smile, which also held a trace of triumph, as she looked at the door to our now not-so-secret passage. In our haste to leave, we had forgotten to close it. We were caught like rats in a trap.

Moments later, Hugo and I were being led into the main hall like trophies and then into the long dining room where we had earlier managed to escape the doctor. We were made to sit back-to-back on a couple of dining room chairs. Mrs Fitzgerald then produced some blue silk cords which, I recognised, had been used to tie back the heavy dining room curtains.

The sun was by now well and truly up and its light pouring into the room from the four long windows which overlooked the back lawns. I could easily see the lines etched across the doctor's forehead which was beaded with sweat, as he tied me roughly to my seat.

Somehow my body had become accustomed to the high levels of adrenaline pumping around it; my fear being replaced by anger.

'What are you going to do with us?' I demanded.

'I would have thought that was pretty obvious, my dear,' the doctor replied, tightening a knot so that the cord cut into my wrists.

'Naturally, my wife and I regret that we won't be able to take you both with us. Our retirement plans do not include you and, besides, we only have two plane tickets.'

'Have you finished, Victor?' Mrs Fitzgerald bellowed from the far end of the room.

'Nearly, my dearest.'

'But why?' I barely heard Hugo ask his captor.

'That's a very good question, Hugo.' The doctor ceased his tightening of the ropes and stood looking at us with a strange look of contempt on his face.

'Do you know who I am?' he continued. 'Everyone knows me as a doctor but my real name isn't Fitzgerald. No, that's my wife's name. We decided, as we were coming here, it would be wiser if I took hers, as it may cause a few problems for us. My real name is Victor Ellington-Smyth. I am your father's cousin and that makes me your second cousin.'

He paused for a few moments in order for his words to sink in.

'And,' he continued, whilst scanning the room with a critical eye, 'all this, by rights, should be mine. But just look what you have all done to it.' He flung out his arms in a theatrical gesture towards the worn, faded carpet and frayed curtains.

'So how do think I have felt all these years, watching you squander what was rightfully mine?'

'But it was your father who caused all the problems in the first place,' Hugo replied courageously.

'That's what your father wants you to believe. At least my father knew how to be Lord of the Manor.'

'What? Spending money like water on lavish parties and selling off farms and making tenants homeless in order to pay for it all.'

'And what exactly has your father done? Look at this place, it's in a disgraceful state. Your family are not fit to be custodians of its rich heritage. The final indignity being to sell it off,' he added, in disgust.

'My father and grandfather did all they could to try and keep this place going and repair some of the damage your father did to the estate—'

'Oh yes, all those hare-brained schemes! The Grouse shoot, the dinner party and what next? Now, I hear he is selling out to a television company. How demeaning. The trouble with your father is that he is too naïve. The key to the ammunition cupboard was too easy to find—'

'You took it!' I could feel Hugo try to move in his chair.

'Yes,' he proudly announced. 'Easy really, just like cancelling the caterers; that only took a phone call.'

'But my father trusted you; he thought of you as his friend.'

'Yes, I know, but then I cultivated that friendship. How else could I have gained his trust? Only then could I plan his downfall to avenge my father.'

'How did you know about the hidden picture?' Hugo asked.

'I didn't, dear boy. It is my good fortune that I saw you two fiddling around with the portrait, so I just stood back and watched. It was good of you to find it for me, but it's no more than I deserve.

'I might ask you how you knew of its existence... but I'm afraid we haven't got time, flights to catch and all that... Veronica, are you ready, my dear?'

'I think so,' the doctor's wife replied. 'Just the finishing touch, which I believe is in your pocket.'

'Ah yes.' The doctor began to feel in his pockets and brought out a box of matches, which he threw in his wife's direction.

We had both been so totally absorbed in what the doctor had told us that I hadn't noticed what his wife had been doing. Looking over my left shoulder towards the fireplace, I could see a large pile of logs had been stacked in the grate; my heart lurched at the sight of one of the long curtains which had been deliberately placed under one of these logs. It was easy to see why; once the fire got going, the curtain would catch fire, the flames would travel to the tapestry wall-hanging above the fireplace and then along the velvet-covered pelmet. The doctor's wife had made sure all the curtains were tied together with the remaining curtain ties, so that the flames could easily cross from one window to the other and engulf the room and us with it.

I heard her strike one of the matches and my fear reached a new level.

'When you are ready, my dear, we must get a move on.'

'You will never get away with it,' Hugo hissed at them.

'Oh, I think we will, dear boy. Try not to worry too much, the smoke should get to you long before the flames.'

We heard them walk out of the room and close the door firmly behind them, against the background sound of wood crackling in the fireplace.

After a few minutes, Hugo started shouting for help, over and over, in a voice I hardly recognised as his own. Unfortunately for us, Mrs B would still be fast asleep at the other end of the house; not only would she be unable to hear us but she wouldn't be up for a couple of hours.

'Listen Hugo.' I decided that blind panic wouldn't solve anything; we needed to think and quickly. 'We must try and get over to the French window. Do you think we could try and jump the chairs towards the window, without tipping ourselves over?'

'We could give it a try.'

'OK, on a count of three. One, two, three...'

Well, we were still upright and with a great deal of effort had managed to move about three centimetres nearer to the window.

'Again, one, two, three...'

Time was passing all too quickly as we inched our way towards the window. And then what? I wasn't sure. The action of jumping our chairs made the ropes dig into our wrists and ankles, causing them to hurt with every movement. Looking to my left, I was horrified to see that the curtain was now alight and as the flames were travelling travelled up towards the pelmet only a short distance away.

We continued our slow progress. I was aiming for a large decorative stand, with a matching pot containing a fern standing on top, which stood next to the window. If we could somehow push that over so that it smashed the glass, we might be able to get out.

It seemed as if we were in a race of some macabre type. As we neared the French door, the flames were also drawing nearer and nearer. Smoke was beginning to fill the room, stinging our eyes and making us cough, but we were just about there.

Moments later, I was positioned in front of the stand; my feet and knees were touching it.

'Right,' I said breathlessly. 'We just need to move forward again and try and push this through the glass. On a count of three. One, two, three...'

Over it went, knocking the plant off the top where it broke into pieces on the floor. The stand itself fell forward onto the glass pane where it smashed through with a loud crash, but there it lodged, about halfway down the window. A draft of clean morning air wafted in through the gap and I inhaled its coolness.

'Has it gone through?' Hugo asked.

'It's not gone all the way down, we must inch forward a bit further and try and push it through,' I replied, trying to sound more optimistic than I felt, as I knew this was going to be a bit tricky as the stand lay at an awkward angle.

'One, two, three...'

We were nearly there, when disaster struck. Our

chairs wobbled as two of the legs struck some of the broken china scattered around the floor at our feet and we toppled over on to our sides. There was one positive outcome; our fall had caused the remainder of the stand to crash through the window, we heard the sound of it breaking on the paving outside and felt the cool breeze on our faces as we lay in this helpless position.

Moments later, panic rising in me like the temperature of the room, I found myself calling for help. Hugo, sensing my alarm, joined in too. I don't know how long we shouted for. It could have been seconds or minutes but, all of a sudden, I was aware of the sound of a crunching sound. At first I thought that it was the sound of the glass crackling from the heat, so it didn't register straight away. Then I noticed that glass was falling on me, forcing me to close my eyes. Next, I was aware of the sound of glass crunching and a pair of strong hands pulling me up. Opening my eyes, I glimpsed a dark tweed jacket tied with string.

'It's alright, Miss, I've got you.' I looked up through my tears and saw Todd's concerned face.

4th September

Sitting up in bed in my pink and green bedroom, I realise how lucky I've been, and also how much in life seem to depend on events we call coincidences. If Todd had not been walking through the Manor garden that morning and heard the sound of the window smashing and our calls for help. If Hugo hadn't invited me around to stay that night. If the doctor hadn't walked into the hall just as we discovered the secret picture and if Lady Carlotta hadn't woken me. What would have happened? But then I don't I believe in coincidences.

The police managed to catch up with the doctor and his wife at the airport and, thankfully, the painting was returned to Hugo's father.

The police and the fire engines arrived very quickly once the alarm had been raised, which is more than could be said for Mrs B; she had to be woken by the police. Apparently she had managed to sleep soundly through the whole thing!

The police questioned us both at the hospital. The only tricky bit was how we discovered the painting.

'We noticed earlier on that a bit of the top canvas

was loose at one of the corners and decided to investigate later what was underneath,' Hugo told them, rather convincingly, I thought.

'Well, that was a bit of luck, wasn't it?' the police inspector said, regarding us both a little suspiciously.

The sound of Mum bounding up the stairs jolted me out of my thoughts.

'Suzann,' she said breathlessly, bursting in through the door. 'Suzann, Hugo is here to see you.'

Mum grabbed my dressing gown and held it for me to put on. I briefly had time to check my appearance in the dressing table mirror as I passed it. I looked a fright. My hair looked like I had had an electric shock and it stuck out in all directions. I was still covered with red scratches where the fallen glass had fallen on me.

'Come on,' Mum urged.

Hugo was waiting in the front room. I saw the flowers before I saw him. He was almost obscured by the biggest bouquet I think have ever seen. I recognised roses, lilies and irises all expertly arranged and wrapped in pretty cellophane tied with a huge pink ribbon. He held them out for me.

'These are for you.'

'Thank you,' I muttered, feeling slightly embarrassed.

'Let me put these in water for you,' Mum said, taking them into the kitchen.

Once Mum had left, an air of awkwardness hung between us. I was conscious of my pink towelling dressing gown and fluffy animal slippers.

Hugo broke the silence first:

'How are you feeling?'

'Fine, what about you?'

'Oh, I'm OK, you got the worst of it with all that glass falling on you.'

'What about the damage to the Manor?'

'Well the dining room is wrecked but structurally it's fine, thank goodness. The television company have said that they will help to restore it, so that it will be ready for when they start filming. Then, of course, there is the painting. Father is getting it valued this week, then he will decide whether to sell it or not.'

'So the Manor is saved then,' I said.

'Yes, it is.' Hugo paused for a few second before continuing. 'I thought you might like to know that Father is going to restore the gatehouse and let Todd use it, in return for a few odd jobs around the place, as there will be a lot to do once work starts, and before the TV company start filming. Perhaps you might like to come and see them in action? I should be back from school by then.'

He turned to go.

'I just came to say...thank you and to ask... I just wondered how... I don't quite understand...' He seemed to struggle to find the right words. 'I always thought there was something different and special about you, and now I know there is.'

*

Later that night, I woke to feel Lily snuggling up to me on the bed. Someone must have left the kitchen door open and she had sneaked upstairs; she purred contentedly.

I could feel the cool night air wafting in through the light curtains causing them to move gently apart, revealing the bright moonlight. Lily suddenly stirred and sat up as I lay there watching silvery beams gently touching various objects around the room. As it shone on my old rocking chair I noticed it rocking rhythmically to and fro due to the breeze, or was it?

I sat up to look more closely and I saw a figure

begin to appear which soon took on a familiar form.

'Hello Suzann.' The loving gaze of my grandmother smiled at me. 'I wasn't able to be with you before love, but, I can now.'

Slowly her image faded into a tiny pool of light before finally disappearing altogether.

*

Hours later, Mum woke me with the news I already knew. Granny May had died in the night.

*

After reading these last two entries in Suzann's diary, Cara reached for her tablet and typed in 'Fire at Durley Manor'. After a couple of seconds, there it was, complete with a black and white photo, showing a blackened, broken French window with three figures standing in a huddle slightly to one side. One Cara recognised from earlier pictures she had seen of him, it was clearly Hugo. She also recognised from the description given, that standing next to him was Todd, but what captivated her the most, was the female figure wrapped in a blanket, standing next to him, although her features were difficult to make out from the grainy old photograph, the open, unsmiling face, framed by a mass of curly hair, seemed to hold

Cara's gaze. She felt, it was without doubt, the face of the author of the diaries she now held in her hands. She felt a shudder go through her. The article said:

'On the night of 2nd of September 1969 a fire, deliberately started by Doctor Fitzgerald, badly damaged the dining room and ancillary rooms at Durley Manor. Lord Easton's son Hugo and friend, were rescued from the blaze by Todd Rowland, of no fixed abode, who was hailed as a hero.'

*

At last she now had a picture of Suzann but, she also had a date, although it was frustrating that they had not printed her name along with Hugo's, perhaps she hadn't wanted the publicity. Cara had to admit to slight pangs of guilt, as she remembered her first thoughts about her diaries were that they were possibly works of fiction. However, if Cara had been honest with herself, she had known, probably from the start that Suzann's diary wasn't a figment of her imagination and hadn't made any of this up. In a way, she hadn't wanted it to be true, because it raised all sorts of questions which were difficult to find answers for.

She also realised that there must be a reason for all that had happened to Cara since moving to the house. All those so-called coincidences, she was sure, had to mean something. Suzann had said herself that there is no such thing as a coincidence, there had to be some connection with Suzann's life and her own. She didn't know what that was and hadn't the faintest idea where to start but, all the same, felt compelled somehow to find out.

*

Cara must have eventually drifted off to sleep only to be awakened suddenly. The moon was shining brightly through a gap in her curtains, casting its silvery light onto her desk and chair, sitting on which, she could clearly see the outline of a figure silhouetted against the moon light.

'Suzann?' Cara asked, instinctively, as she slowly sat up to get a better look. But it disappeared, leaving Cara wondering what she had just seen.